SHIFTERS

Have an adventure!

Halli Lilburn

Halli Lilburn

SHIFTERS

http://www.hallililburn.blogspot.com

FIRST EDITION trade paperback

Imajin Books

May 30, 2012

ISBN: 978-1-926997-68-1

Art & cover designed by Mitchell Davidson Bentley, Atomic Fly Studios - http://www.atomicflystudios.net

Praise for Shifters

"In Halli Lilburn's sci-fi adventure, *Shifters*, a group of elite students traverse a minefield of alternate realities to discover there's one enduring thing worth fighting for—their freedom." —Judith Graves, author of the SKINNED series

"A spellbinder that captures the reader on the first page. Eerily insightful and possible, chilling." —Christina Francine, *Midwest Book Review*

"*Shifters* is more than just a YA book. It's a book that causes you to stop and think about the way that we view anyone who is different than us. It will move you and have you turning the pages." —Jeff Rivera, author of *Forever My Lady*

To my genius children.
May your imaginations never diminish.

Acknowledgements

I have to thank the NaNoWriMo people for urging me to be one of the 18% who actually finish.

I also have to thank my family for putting up with me staying in bed and typing all day.

Thank you to my SCBWI critique group and April for cheering me on.

Thank you to the crew at Imajin for all of their help.

Prologue

"You have to get out of here," Coach Tyler whispered as the last of the swim team students shuffled out the door.

I stopped treading water, grabbed the edge of the pool and stared at my swim coach. "What do you mean? Don't I have extra practice today?"

"That's not what I'm talking about." His ominous words matched the fear in his eyes.

Was he saying I had to leave the school? My suspicions had been building since the moment I got here. Security guards crowded the hallways, surveillance cameras adorned the buildings and a detection gate stood guard at every doorway.

"It's not just the school." Coach Tyler paused as a student came out of the locker room and went outside. His eyes lingered on the door. "It's everywhere." He gave me a moment to process his words.

I took my goggles off and set them on the edge of the pool. I tucked a piece of unruly red hair under my swim cap.

He crouched down. "Miss Pawlak—Halina—you can't be here anymore. You've compromised your standing. You have to leave."

I was a good swimmer, but that wasn't the only reason I had joined the swim team. I had ulterior motives for wanting to be near Coach Gerome Tyler. I could feel his eyes staring into my soul. He stood so near, but for all the wrong reasons. He was blond, blue-eyed and young enough to expect an infatuation or two from his teenage students—me included. His close proximity elicited an intense fluttery feeling under my sternum. I had to snap out of it. This was not the time for a crush rush.

"Listen," I said, "I know I've missed a couple of curfews and practices, but I think kicking me out is unjustified and—"

"I'm not expelling you."

Silence again.

What was I supposed to be reading into this? Surely he didn't know what my friends and I had really been up to. Or did he?

"It's the whole planet." Coach Tyler raked his hands through his surfer hair. "The Special Force is not what you think it is."

I already knew that. The Special Force was the mother of all conspiracies.

Chapter 1

I felt the first waves of warning when we received the *Guidelines and Stipulations Manual* from Principal Arter. At opening assembly of our first year, I sat with my friends as we received the file on our phones. We flipped through the manual in silence.

Arter loomed over the microphone and his droopy cheeks swayed when he talked. "Welcome to Young Adult Collegiate—or YAC for short. The Special Force of Canada has created this amalgamation of high school and college to allow you to specialize sooner and graduate an expert in your field of study. You have all undergone rigorous screening tests because YAC only accepts the best and brightest."

"Rigorous is right," my pal Yusef whispered. "My parents bent over backward to get me here. I'm lucky they could afford it."

I nudged him. "I would have freaked if you hadn't been accepted." Our teachers in our advanced classes back home probably gave us gushy letters of recommendation, praising our credentials and conveniently forgetting to mention our liabilities. I bet they were pretty tired of us and glad to see us go. The lot of us could be troublesome at times.

"You have been given the guidelines and stipulations," Arter continued, "that are compulsory for your entrance qualifications. I hope you take them very seriously."

Through the thousands of faces in the auditorium, I swear Arter was staring right at me.

Glynis, my sassy Aussie friend, thumbed through the text on her phone. "Are we the only ones that can see how wrong this is? The curfew I can understand. They need to keep a good rep, but the detection gates and ID imprints are a bit much."

Instead of giving us a pass card, they wanted to insert a tattoo under our skin.

"Apparently my parents are so blinded with school pride that they already gave the go-ahead for this." Jan frowned. "We can be scanned, whether we want it or not."

"I'm an independent student, so they didn't have to ask my parents." Torvald flexed his neck muscles, showing off to Glynis. "Of course, if I don't consent, I'm no longer allowed in."

Yusef ran his brown hands through his black hair. "This is the beginning of the end."

Jan squinted her Asian eyes. "The end of what?"

"The end of education and the beginning of prison."

At the time, I thought Yusef was being a bit overdramatic.

The procedure was painless. When it was over, everyone had an iridescent silver bar on the left side of the neck. It was a faint but constant reminder that the school kept tabs on our every move.

When we walked into class, we passed through a detection gate that registered our attendance. Gates into the dorms prevented us from breaking curfew. The imprints also held data in memory. Anytime the professors wanted to know our marks, they would scan our necks with a little portable screen.

Being the genius that he was, Yusef found a way to crash their system.

"It's a revolution," he said.

He figured out simple ways around the system, including the detection gates. The doors were able to tattle on us, but the windows weren't. A major oversight on Arter's part. Sneaking out of windows was a time-honoured tradition. The split-level dorms provided a short climb up a trellis, making it a cinch to sneak out to the late show or for Glynis to see her guy after hours.

We got caught a couple of times and Principal Arter lectured us about attitude and respect. Nothing we hadn't heard before, though the threat of expulsion was scarier knowing this school qualified as a postsecondary institution. We wanted freedom, but not at the cost of our future careers.

"Let this be a lesson to you kids." Arter pointed a rubbery finger at my face, singling me out yet again. "If I catch you out of your dorms past curfew one more time, it will mean suspension."

He was scary. Every time he looked at me, it was like the devil himself was biding his time before he dragged me down to hell.

As we left Arter's office, I saw my pal Spencer waiting for his turn.

His usual toothy grin was surprisingly absent.

"So, Spence, what did you do?" I plopped down on the bench beside him.

He didn't answer. He stared at the floor, miserable.

"Is something wrong?" I coaxed.

"My calculus prof failed me."

"How can they fail you? The semester isn't even over."

"Apparently it doesn't have to be. I didn't even get a warning."

"Well, can't you try again next year?"

"Not at this school. I've been expelled."

"Just for failing Calculus?" I exploded. "One class? I've never heard anything so idiotic in my life. This is wrong. Unfair."

What did they think they would gain with such high expectations?

"My mom's gonna kill me." Spence hung his head and kicked the bench.

I knew his mom. Spence and I used to go trick or treating together. I helped him make his costumes. He would hide his candy at my house so that his mom wouldn't catch him, and I would bring an extra piece to school for him every day.

Arter's office door opened. "Spencer Wright, your time has come."

Again the association with the grim reaper. What was up with this man?

I touched Spencer's shoulder. "It'll be okay."

He nodded, but said nothing as he shuffled into the room.

As soon as Arter's door shut, Yusef steered us down to the computer lab.

"What are you doing?" I asked.

"I've had enough of this. I'm on a mission to hack into the school network and wreck something."

We all gathered in the lab while he did a little illegal research. We came to support him, although we didn't really know what he was doing. Jan and I checked our network messages while Torvald and Glynis snuggled at the desk behind us. The snowy, Edmonton winter swirled outside the window.

"How's the fitness program coming, Yusef?" Torvald talked about what he knew best. Torvald had taken Yusef under his wing and started him on a personal fitness plan.

"Love the challenge, Tor, but I'm still as skinny as ever."

We all laughed.

Yusef refocused on the matter at hand. The monitor lit up his face while he clicked away on the mouse. "I don't understand why I can't find anything. It's as if their system is completely isolated."

I sat at the computer beside him. "I don't see how that would be practical. How do the teachers submit marks or attendance records? How can a school function without this stuff?"

He shrugged. "The detection gates must be keeping a tally on some hard drive somewhere. I'm going to find it and find out why it's such a big secret."

"Maybe they do it the old-fashioned way and chisel it into a slab of rock." Torvald leaned over the desk. He draped his majorly buff arm around Glynis's shoulders.

Glynis licked her lips and squeezed Torvald's biceps. She had tied up her streaky blond hair in a messy knot. "Well, something around here sure is chiselled," she said with a thick Australian accent.

We rolled our eyes. As per usual with those two.

Jan turned to Yusef. "What about their website? Doesn't that at least have our profiles on it?"

"Yeah, except all that information gets updated here manually by the students."

"That seems archaic and time consuming."

I had to agree with Jan. Back home we used to have our own blog pages connected with the school's site. Monitors shut down any site that had inappropriate material. After a while, so many pages had been deleted that the school abandoned the whole idea. I wasn't surprised when YAC refused to provide any type of online social program for the students, not even a messenger service.

Yusef's research recovered nothing about YAC—no blueprints for the buildings and no architect. The construction contracts had been done in-house within Special Force and they weren't available either. Nobody could tell us where the school kept the mainframe. It was as if it didn't exist. So

Yusef gave us all cartography assignments to map out the school and find a supposedly hidden room. "We can measure by counting steps," he said. "That way no one will know what we're doing."

We silently counted steps on the way to class. We calculated steps from one wall to another, despite puzzled expressions from our peers. Soon we had everything drawn out—windows, doors, closets, stairways. Skipping class was the best way to get a lecture, which gave us a chance to survey the teachers' private offices.

Yusef put his graphics skills to good use and came up with diagrams of every square inch of YAC. Still, nothing showed up, as if the mainframe and all of its secrets had been sucked into another dimension.

Chapter 2

Summers in Victoria were the best. I appreciated it even more now that I had spent a winter on the cold prairies. The ocean brought fresh, warm winds to the island. Everyone's lawns had the greenest grass and an overabundance of flowers. Every once in a while, a hummingbird would show up at the birdfeeder outside my window.

I tried to sleep in those first couple of days, but my body couldn't break out of its early morning schedule. I took the opportunity to come downstairs and eat breakfast with the folks before they both went off to work. Dad was sitting reading the paper and Mom was making a breakfast bagel. The sun shone through the lacy curtains, casting shadows from the hollyhocks growing outside.

"Halina, dear, can I make you breakfast? If you want to go out today, I'll leave you some spending money." Mom passed me a bagel and then snapped her fingers at my dad until he passed me a twenty from under his paper. My parents were great.

"Mom, what did Spencer's parents say when he got sent home?" I asked between bites. I wanted an update on his situation before I called over there. I needed to ensure that whatever punishment his parents had given him for the expulsion wasn't going to interfere with my plans to hang out. His mother was a constant stick in the mud.

"Hasn't anyone told you?" Mom put her breakfast bagel down on the plate in front of her.

"Told me what?"

"They didn't even announce it at school?" Dad peered over his paper. "I'm calling Principal Arter. When something like this happens, the rest of the kids have a right to know, even if he's no longer a student."

He tossed down his napkin and straightened his tie.

It was the first time I'd heard him express a negative comment about the school.

"What happened?" I looked to Mom again.

"Honey..." She only called me honey if it was bad news. "Spencer went missing a few weeks after he was rejected from YAC. His parents have been looking for him for over a month."

I was shocked. "Why didn't you tell me? Spencer has been my neighbour most of my life. How could he be missing?"

"Mrs. Wright did call the school. Principle Arter called a general assembly."

"No, he didn't." I paused. "I...I'm going over there." I left the table with my breakfast still sitting there.

"That would be nice. Mrs. Wright could use some cheering up." Mom cleared away my plate.

That wasn't my reasoning, though I didn't say anything.

I walked down the old street looking at the mature elm trees on either side. Bright blue-green moss clutched the corrugated bark. The fingers of branches nearly touched each other in the middle, giving the road the appearance that it covered the sky with a net of leaves arching overhead.

A chill pulled at my scalp. I ran my fingers through my curls, but the shiver didn't subside. I couldn't push out the thought that the school had something to do with Spencer's disappearance.

Five houses down, I rang the bell. Mrs. Wright answered the door in her housecoat, looking tired and dishevelled.

"Oh, Halina, how have you been?"

"What happened?" I asked.

She slumped. "You better come in. I've just made some tea."

The living room had heavy curtains drawn, leaving it shaded despite the sunshine outside. A desk in the corner was crowded with computers, tracking devices and at least three phones. A stack of long posters sat on the floor. I read the page on top.

MISSING: Spencer Wright. Age 17. Born December 15, 1993. Height 6 feet. Brown hair. Blue eyes. Last seen in his house on Portland Lane, Victoria, B.C. If you have any information regarding his whereabouts, contact the Victoria Police.

I stopped reading. At the bottom was his picture with the huge smile that was so typical of Spencer. I squeezed my eyes shut and pinched the bridge of my nose. It all felt so unreal.

"We've done everything we can." Mrs. Wright held out a dainty teacup for me. "The police have come up with nothing."

I took the cup and blew across the hot liquid. We sat down on two antique rocking chairs opposite each other with a glass coffee table between us. It was hard to think of something to say. I sipped my tea for a moment. She had probably already heard words of comfort from so many others. She had probably told the story to a million people. I figured I might as well be blunt.

"Do you think he's dead?" I asked.

She already had an answer to this harsh question. She didn't hesitate. "No, oh no, the police don't suspect foul play and if he had an accident, we would have found him by now. He never went anywhere without telling me."

I smirked. Little did she know.

"I think he is a runaway," she continued. "He was always threatening that he would leave. He was always so defiant—never very stable."

"Stable? What is that supposed to mean?" I raised an eyebrow.

"Come on now, Halina, surely you noticed. He had a real problem following a regular schedule. He opposed authority. Smart, but he could have done so much better if he put his mind to it. Getting kicked out of Young Adult Colligate was the straw that broke the camel's back."

"Are you sure that's what did it?" I shouldn't have said that aloud, but I was done being superficially respectful. I hid my face behind my cup as I tipped it back, building up some courage to speak out against her. I gulped the rest of the tea even though it burned my throat.

"Pardon me? What did you say?"

"Maybe that preverbal straw had to do with the fact that he had to come back here and face you."

"Yes, he was probably overwhelmed with shame." She slowly shook her head, turning her teacup in her hands.

I bit my lip. That was not what I meant. Why would he want to stick around and deal with a mother who was constantly degrading him? Even when we were kids, she had unattainable expectations. I didn't tell her about the assembly that never happened. I put my empty cup down on the coffee table.

It made her cringe to see my cup on the bare glass. "It was hard enough getting him to put forth the effort to make it into that school in the first place."

"Well, I hope he is somewhere better than here. Somewhere he can be happy."

She sucked in a tiny squeak. This time she understood my meaning all right. She glared as if her eyes could punish me. "I think you should leave."

"Of course you do." I got up. If Spence had run away, I could see the reason why. Good for him. Still, it bothered me that nobody had heard from him or seen him. Where had he gone?

Spence wasn't one of my best buds. However, I figured *someone* would hear from him. If he was going to call someone, it wouldn't be me, but it might be Yusef.

"Maybe he's changed his identity. You know, like the witness protection program." Yusef was tapping at his computer, searching Spencer's name. He had been at it for an hour. Nothing helpful had come up.

"Well, can you find out?" I asked.

"I could, but I'm not going to. That would be illegal." He said *illegal* in slow motion like his brother Ibram always did. Ibram, the con man, was sneaking us into a gig later that night.

Giving up on the search for Spencer was hard to do. I had to admit it, we were getting nowhere.

I grabbed the mouse from him and clicked on shut down. "Come on, computer geek, let's get ready."

He stood up. "I'm not a computer geek. I don't go to Star Trek conventions, I don't download music illegally and I especially don't hack into police files or the CSIS database. I just like computers. My idea of fun is taking cute chicks out dancing. A computer geek doesn't do that."

"Well, I'll never make that mistake again." I crossed my heart. "Come on, I don't want to be late for The Consonant C. They are one of my favourite indie-tronica groups."

We were decked out in our finest. Jan had on Kabuki make-up. Glynis dyed her hair bright pink. Torvald flew out from E-town for the occasion. I backcombed my hair until it piled on my head like a curly pom-pom. Yusef had a black toque pulled right down to his eyes and his pants were nearly falling off. It was our first break-in to a no-minors gig. The halls in Edmonton scanned our imprints to check our birthdates, making it impossible to sneak in. The city wanted to expand the use of the imprints to include banking information and purchasing. Luckily, Victoria hadn't caught onto that fad yet and this hall used old-fashioned paper tickets to pass through the doors. Ibram and Torvald went ahead of us with five other friends, all of whom had legit tickets. Once they were inside, he collected their ticket stubs and brought them out for us to 'recycle.' It was as easy as pie.

Chapter 3

"It must be a secret door," Jan said when we got back from summer holidays. "It seems silly, but it's the only logical explanation."

The search for a secret door and a hidden computer system became our first assignment of the new semester.

My first year gave me ample time to be noticed by Coach Tyler. Sure enough, he called me over when practices resumed.

I shivered—and not just from the water evaporating on my skin.

"Miss Pawlak." His voice was usually commanding when he coached. This time it was more relaxed.

"Yes, sir." I blinked the dripping water out of my eyes to keep a better gaze on him. He couldn't be more than twenty-two. That was only five years older than I was—hardly criminal.

"I have noticed a great improvement in your concentration. You seem more determined, more dedicated."

"Thank you." My teeth chattered a bit and he handed me a towel.

"I think with a little more effort you could be ready to compete in the Summer Games in July."

Maybe that was encouragement. Maybe not. He expected me to be flattered.

Just to impress him, I made it look like I was. "That would be great." I faked a happy smile. Whatever it took.

"I'm wondering if you would be willing to stay after practice for some extra coaching."

"From you?"

"Yes, of course."

My mind began tossing out imaginative motivations. I drew a

picture of him and me together in our swimsuits with no one else in the pool, and the sun setting through the big picture windows.

"What about Fridays?" I suggested.

"I only work here on Tuesdays and Thursdays. No exceptions. It will push your limits to add an extra hour to your practices, but I think that will be the kind of conditioning you need."

"Have you asked anyone else on the team?" Not that I was jealous, I just wondered about crowd control.

"Just you so far."

I knew I wasn't the best on the team. He hadn't picked me for my skill and that must mean something. He must have picked me for *other* reasons.

The extra practices were hard. We did water rescue training as well as prepare for the Summer Games. I pushed myself, hoping that my dedication would impress him. If he was trying to hint at a relationship, I never caught it. Still, I clung to some hope that he would confess his love to me any day. In the meantime, he was hot and I got to spend time with him. The downside was I had less time with my friends. I came back to the dorms exhausted after practice. That meant less late shows and fewer evil eyes from the principal.

With the extra practices, I hardly had time for myself, let alone Yusef's quest to find the magical secret door to his vengeful crash project. But I didn't have to find it, because Jan did.

We were walking to our Logic class together when Jan stopped in the middle of the hall. Her almond eyes narrowed to black slits.

"What are you staring at?" I looked in the same direction. I didn't see anything exceptional.

"The ped-way," she said.

Yes, of course. The ped-way that reached across a courtyard from the main building to the fitness centre.

"The mainframe is in the ped-way."

I looked again. The walls were glass, and we could see students with gym bags walking across. We had already counted steps on the ped-way. We hadn't counted the height of the ped-way. Above the corridor, where a sloping roof should have been, there was enough space for an attic. A secret room.

"Good job, girl," I said as we sped toward the fitness centre. Running up a flight of stairs, we began feeling the walls for grooves. Students passed us, too focused on getting to class to notice our odd behaviour.

"Lina!" Jan startled herself with her shout and she covered her mouth. She lowered her voice. "I've got something."

I slipped in front of some guys coming up the stairs and smiled awkwardly as an apology for cutting them off.

"Look right in the frame of the first window."

I saw it. The frame had designs in the wood, small rectangles cut with a router. The indentations went in about a centimetre. One of them at about knee level cut all the way through the frame. The grain in the wood wasn't even the same.

"You girls will be late for class." We both sucked in a breath as we became aware that Coach Tyler was standing at the top of the stairs. I stood up, feeling like a jewel thief caught red-handed. Jan remained crouched with her back to him.

"What are you doing?" he asked.

I had no answer except a silent, open mouth.

Jan quickly thought of a cover-up. "I-I just dropped my cell phone." She mimed putting it back in her purse. "Sorry, we'll try not to be late." She grabbed me and we ran across the ped-way.

I snuck a peek back to see if Mr. Tyler was looking at us. If he knew about the secret door, I figured he would acknowledge it in some way. Instead, he just turned and left. Maybe he didn't know about it either. Maybe we got away.

That night Yusef and Torvald came climbing up the trellis to our window.

"Hey, girls." Torvald's booming voice brought Glynis prancing over from across the hall. She practically jumped on him when she came through the door. They always got in a little make-out time whenever they were away from Glynis's roommate, Paula, who wouldn't even let them hold hands in front of her. We just rolled our eyes and told them to go in the bathroom or something.

Besides the magnet-mouths, the rest of us were single. Yusef had shown interest in Jan a couple of years ago, though she'd made it very clear that she was a career woman with enough meat on her plate to forgo any other persona besides tough tank-chick. Even if nothing ever got started, he kept hanging close, glad to be friends with us.

Jan was at her computer typing like a mad woman.

"What are you working on?" I asked.

"My quantum mechanics assignment from Professor Petersen." Clickety clack.

"So, are you going to try explaining String Theory or are you playing it safe to get brownie points?"

She scrunched up her eyebrows. "I hate it when you put it like that. The micro universe cannot be compared to the macro universe. Just because I'm agreeing with Petersen doesn't make me a brown-noser." She flipped her braids over her shoulder.

"Sure it does." Yusef looked up from his phone. "But it would impress her more if you proved her wrong."

"Easier said than done, hon. How do you describe a particle smaller than ten to the thirty-fifth power? How can it change shape? What's powering it? What lies in the space between each string?"

"A vacuum." I said. "A void of dark matter."

"That's the problem with you theorists. You can make up whatever sounds scientifically plausible without precedent and you never have to prove it. There is nothing between the strings unless there is another dimension. If vacuums were embedded in every atom then what would prevent us from getting sucked inside ourselves and popping out the other end? No one can study that."

Yusef put his phone down. "We're not talking about massive amounts of gravity like a black hole. We aren't condensing mass, we are shifting it. Like magnetism. The Strong Force theory acts like opposing charges, propelling mirrored matter into another dimension.."

"But this isn't dealing with magnetism, it's dealing with energy." she argued.

"Same thing." I said.

"Ugh. I hate quantum mechanics." She growled at her screen then deleted the entire page. "I need to get out of here."

I got up and banged on the bathroom door. "Come on guys, detach yourselves. Let's go."

The moon was high and bright as we silently snuck across the courtyard toward the ped-way. The notch in the window frame pushed in easily, popping out a panel in the wall. Our flashlights revealed a narrow staircase leading to the space above the ped-way. A faint blue glow was coming from the top.

"Bingo," said Yusef as he climbed the stairs. We all followed.

The room was a dark corridor running the length of the ped-way. Along one wall, shone a blue, glowing machine that I assumed was the mainframe. It didn't look like any computer I'd ever seen. Seeing the blank expression on Yusef's face, I could guess that he had never seen anything like it either. That same iridescent silver as our imprints flowed over the screen like a slow moving waterfall of plasma, but it was dry when we touched it. The keyboard had hundreds of extra keys with odd symbols. As soon as Yusef put his fingers to the keys, a message floated out of the moving waterfall, *Unknown User.*

"Is that a challenge?" Torvald had this running joke about unauthorized personalities only. His joke circulated around campus—like painted on the staff room door.

Yusef's face lit up and he began to concentrate in earnest.

I turned to study the room more carefully. It made me feel like we were in some kind of sci-fi dream. Like the odd apparatuses mounted on the wall and the tall glass tubes full of small black hockey pucks. Well, they looked like hockey pucks. I stretched my hand out to the glass that dissolved as I touched it, allowing me to grab one of the pucks It was the size of a small button, but thicker. A series of six numbers were engraved on it, the same on both sides—837120.

I looked at a collection of syringes and needles that could morph into different widths as if they were made of expanding clear rubber. One syringe had the silver stuff inside. The serum they used to make our imprints. I squeezed a little bit out onto my hand, but it evaporated instantly.

Glynis, who wasn't all that into digit-tech, looked doubtfully at the screen. "Is this even a computer, mate? It looks more like a lava-lamp."

"Of course it is." Yusef pointed at the screen and it morphed into a list of numbers. "Otherwise I couldn't do this."

A message floated out. *Welcome to the Real Administration System. RAS.*

"I didn't even think this kind of thing had been invented yet," he said. "It's like a touch screen, only better. It can sense where you are looking and enlarges that section to see it better. I bet it even has audio response."

A sickly-sweet female voice with an Irish accent said, "Audio response activated. Welcome to the Real Administration System."

Torvald gave a low whistle. The most he knew about computers was how to run his iPod during his fitness training.

"Show me student profiles. Specifically, Yusef Hassam." Yusef's picture and a long list of numbers came floating out of the waterfall, as well as a list of all his classes, attendance, marks and every other piece of info they had on him. At the very top were two stats in bold.

Location: RAS/ Ped-Way Entrance 11/05/2012 – 11:58 pm
Status: Stationary 047829

"What does that mean?" Jan pointed toward the words and numbers and the computer magnified them.

"Yusef Hassam is the current user," the voice said. "Yusef Hassam has been scanned. A Stationary Status implies that Yusef Hassam has never shifted from Reality 047829."

I blinked. Shifted from reality? What kind of malarkey statement was that?

We were dumfounded.

"Show me the profiles with a non-stationary status," Yusef said.

All the teachers' faces floated out. I gasped when I saw Coach Tyler, his status labelled *Shifter*.

I stepped forward and blurted out, "Show me status history of Gerome Tyler." His face magnified and a series of numbers began scrolling down the screen. Two particular numbers kept interchanging with a date and time beside each.

047829 – 11/05/2012 - 8:01 am
346181 – 11/05/2012 - 17:49 pm
047829 – 11/07/2012 - 7:58 am
346181 – 11/07/2012 - 19:12 pm

It went on.

"Is this an attendance log?" I asked

"Negative. This is a Real Status log."

"Show me attendance log."

Another series of the same dates popped up with times showing him entering the swimming pool before each practice and leaving sometime after.

Fitness Centre/NW Exterior Door 11/05/2011 - 8:01 am
Ped-way/W Entrance 11/05/2012 - 11:53 am
Ped-way/E Entrance 11/05/2012 - 11:54 am
Cafeteria/N Entrance 11/05/2012 - 11:58 am

Weird. It was a giant surveillance record of everybody who had these stupid ID imprints. They might as well just put collars and leashes on us.

"So much for the *Protection of Personal Privacy Act*." Besides our mutual Logics and Physics classes, Jan was also studying law. "I wonder if the government knows what the Special Force is doing to the educational system in this country—and who knows what else."

"Right now, I would worry less about that and more about the fact that we are about to get caught." Yusef had brought his own file backup and enlarged the location again.

RAS/ Ped-Way Entrance 11/05/2012 – 11:58 pm.

"The mainframe. They know I'm in here. They know we're all in here." Pictures of our faces popped up showing the same location. A detection gate hung over the secret door.

"Now what?" Jan asked.

"This is a long shot, but I'll try it," Yusef said. "Delete last location."

Miraculously, it worked. The locations all switched to *Ped-way*. He tinkered a bit more until the screen showed we were all safely tucked into our beds.

"Hey, good job. That could be useful. We wouldn't have to sneak through the windows anymore." Torvald's grip around Glynis's waist tightened. Yusef muttered something sceptical under his breath and then announced it was probably time to go.

"I'll need a month to figure this all out." He tried to shut down the computer, but the voice spoke up again.

"Shut-down cannot commence until the removal of Plug 837120 is authorized."

"What?"

"Shut-down cannot commence until removal of Plug 837120 is authorized."

Yusef turned. "Okay, what did you guys touch?"

"Lina took something from one of those glass tubes," Glynis said, pointing to the black mini-puck in my hand. Sure enough it had the number 837120 etched on the back.

"Halina Pawlak does not have authorization to remove Plug 837120." The sugary voice was beginning to bother me.

"Can't I just put it back?" I asked.

"Certainly." The tone in her voice made me wonder if this computer was capable of condescension.

I walked back over to the tubes. There must have been thousands of those plugs stacked on top of each other. The glass disintegrated at my touch and I wedged the plug back into place. As soon as I let go, the glass grew back into place as if nothing had disturbed it.

"That is freaky," I said, pointing at the glass.

"This whole thing is freaky with a capital F," Glynis added.

"Commencing shut-down."

"We hope you enjoyed flying with us." Jan mimicked the artificial voice, turning her into a flight attendant.

Everyone chuckled. We snuck out as our faces on the screen melted into a river of glowing blue plasma. As we tiptoed across the courtyard back to our dorms, we congratulated each other on another mission accomplished. Still, we were unsettled. Our little moment of recon-espionage had opened up a whole new bucket of worms. What the heck was going on? What did all of that mean? What exactly was a *Shifter* and why was Coach Tyler one of them?

Chapter 4

"I'm not talking about school. I mean the planet." Coach Tyler was whispering even though we were the only ones at the pool. I squinted at him in doubt, climbing out of the water and pulling my towel around me.

"The Special Force doesn't just exist in Canada. They are infiltrating other governments under different names and guises. The U.S. is using the ID imprints instead of dog tags for their military because some Shifter showed them how useful they would be—"

"Wait, you lost me. What is a Shifter?" Our after-practice discussion was making less and less sense.

He straightened his back, "Don't pretend I don't know where you've been, Halina. If I were you I'd be more discreet about it before Principal Arter finds out."

So he did know. I thought we *were* being discreet about it. Judging by his assumptions, he thought I knew what it all meant. He was giving me more credit than I deserved. He was unaware of the others who were with me last night because I was the only one who left evidence he had found. He must have thought I was a super genius if I did all of that on my own.

"How did you know?" After no response, I continued. "My last location was deleted."

"Halina, you are obviously very bright to have found RAS in the first place, but you've got to cover your tracks. You didn't delete the last user of the plug you took. Luckily, I found it and deleted it for you before anyone else noticed. The Special Force is recruiting kids for their Over-Ride Project. Do you want to become one of their clones, or do you want to get expelled and then go missing just like your friend Spencer did? I care about you enough to stop that from happening." To emphasize his point, he did something amazing. He reached out and took my hands in his.

It sucked my breath away. He cared about me. He was touching me. After all the time and effort I put into impressing him, was it finally paying off? I stared wide-eyed at his hands holding mine, reminding myself to breathe. *What were we talking about?*

"Uh," was all I could say.

"I need you to be safe." Coach Tyler stepped closer and put one hand on my shoulder. "Stop fiddling around with RAS, and if you do start shifting you've got to make sure you don't get caught."

I blinked. I needed to get control of my adrenaline-boosted heart. Something he was saying triggered a red flag in my mind, but I couldn't comprehend it through this crush rush. He was talking about a huge conspiracy project if he just said what I think he said. Was Special Force the cause of Spencer's disappearance?

I opened my mouth to speak and then closed it again. I had to think, and my brain had officially stopped working when he touched me. I pulled my hands away reluctantly. "Okay." I turned to go, brooding over this information overload.

"Wait. You may need this." Coach Tyler put a black plug in my hand. "If you're going to shift, this one is safe. Use it only if you get into a situation you can't get out of. And don't let anyone catch you with it." I looked down at the thick, black button in my hand. I read the numbers—346181.

He didn't explain himself. He just turned and left.

I should have gone straight back to my friends and told them everything Coach Tyler had said. I should have warned them that what we were doing was dangerous. Yusef probably could have explained to me what all that crap was about the Over-Ride Project. I should have told him. Instead, I went to the computer lab and Googled Spencer's name.

Spencer Wright, 17 years of age, went missing from his south-side Victoria home on June 2. After four months of searching, police say they have no leads. Search and rescue teams have been watching the shorelines in case a body washes up. Wright had recently been expelled from The Young Adult Collegiate: a Special Force Institution in Edmonton, Alberta. His parents hopes are fading. "His school meant everything to him," Mrs. Wright told police. "He was devastated."

Yeah, right, Mrs. Wright.

"He was so depressed when YAC rejected him, he became suicidal. I fear the worst," Mrs. Wright said as tears flowed down her cheeks.

That just didn't sound like him at all. Being depressed was one of the last things he was. Did his mother not know her son, or was she lying through her teeth, transferring blame to cover up bad parenting?

I read further. *If you have any information on the whereabouts of Spencer Wright, please contact the Victoria Police Department.*

Unbelievable. On a whim, I tried Googling another student who had failed last year and never came back. What was her name again? Loni...Pitcher. Another news report was at the top of the search list. *Ex-YAC student goes missing.* The paper was the Toronto Star.

"That is really weird," I whispered to myself, unaware if I might be disturbing other students. I nudged the girl beside me. "Hey," I whispered, "do you know the name of a student who dropped out or was expelled last year?"

She exaggerated a sigh and turned from her work. "Yeah, there was a guy in my Literature class. Clive Navien."

I typed in the name. My heart thudded in my chest. The Winnipeg Reporter's title page had a big picture of Clive with *Child Find* written under his face. I didn't even read it. Seeing three ex-students and three missing persons reports was a mountain of evidence something was seriously wrong. It was time to go tell the others.

Chapter 5

"Explain Over-Ride Project," I said.

This time I was sitting at the computer, giving her orders while the others looked on. Pages of text came flowing out of the screen.

The computer's voice grated my nerves. "Over-Ride Project was initiated by Special Force in several different realities. Their goal is to create a superior human species through processes of eliminating weak candidates." She stopped. She was blunt, as if that was all there was to say.

"This is unreal." Jan was red in the face with anger. "This is genocide. What gives them the right—"

"Define unfit candidate." Yusef interrupted her before she exploded.

The voice droned on. "All candidates are put through a screening process. Judges determine if their DNA is corrupted, thus unfit for integration into the human species. They are labelled undesirable."

"Define corrupt DNA."

"That decision is left up to the judges."

"Is Principal Arter a judge?"

"Affirmative."

"Show me all students who have been judged to have corrupt DNA."

Faces floated out of the screen. Among them were Spencer Wright, Loni Pitcher and Clive Navien. In fact, every face that came up was that of an expelled student. We all gasped. Each one of them had the same words written above their heads.

Location: Exile 008610.
Status: Shifter.

We stood in front of the RAS computer with our mouths gaping. The corridor was dark except the pale blue light shining in our eyes.

"I need to show you guys something." I removed the plug from my pocket. "Coach Tyler said I might need this and not to get caught with it. He knew I was in here."

"This is royally messed up." Yusef ran his fingers through his black hair and stared at me. "Why would he give you that? Why does he think you'll need it and what is it for?"

"I don't know. I thought you would know. You know computers better than anyone."

We all waited for his answer.

"I don't know. It's some kind of memory chip with a program on it. It has no port, so it needs a scanning device to work."

"Do you think our imprints could scan it?" I brought the plug up.

"No. Are you stupid?" Yusef grabbed the plug out of my hand. "You can't do that. If our imprints are scanners, they're catalysts to some inter-dimensional portal. Remember Petersen's String Theory assignment? You'll be transported through microcosmic vortexes into another universe or something. Then how will you get back?"

My heart jumped into my throat. If anyone else had said that, I would have laughed and called it a pile of BS, but Yusef didn't advocate nonsense like this. Not unless he believed it was true.

"Wouldn't our Prof be surprised if it actually worked?" Torvald said.

"Darling." Glynis chided, "everyone would be surprised."

"Look at all this." Yusef waved his hand over the desk. "Someone invented this and that means it already works. Someone has shifted out of this universe and figured out how to return. If they can do it safely, we can too."

"You know I think this is way over our heads," Jan was almost whispering. "We should just go back to our dorms and act like we never found this...stuff. If we get caught, we're not just talking expulsion. We are going to disappear like those other kids. This is not cool."

"I don't think those other kids knew about RAS and the ability to shift between universes," Glynis said. "They disappeared for other reasons. Some lame discriminatory teacher decided they weren't cool enough to integrate with the human race and sent them packing to some colony for rejects so the world could be left with some snobby elitist clique."

The two of them started debating the danger we were all in while Yusef and I turned back to the screen.

He tuned them out. "Before we test this, we have to take

precautions. There has to be two plugs. One to get you there and one to get you back." He addressed the computer, "Show me the plug for this reality."

"Plug for Reality 047829 is not available."

"Define not available."

"Plug for Reality 047829 is in use. It was removed by Gerome Tyler at *oh-seven-hundred*."

I gasped. I didn't know what it all meant, but I would find out.

"Sounds like your favourite swim coach is keeping some nasty secrets." Torvald smirked.

"We don't know what this means," I replied. "It could be some harmless game."

"Or a satanic cult with alien technology plotting to take over the world," he remarked.

"You watch too many movies," I muttered. "We need to tell somebody about this."

"What would you tell them and who could you trust?" Jan asked. "This is a government conspiracy. Probably an international project. We are trapped in it."

She sounded crazy. It was freaking me out.

Everyone started arguing. Flabbergasted by the entire situation, I needed more information before I could assess if we were in real danger or not. Jan had already determined that we were. Yusef was still shocked by the existence of this extreme technology. Glynis was ready to butt heads with the first person she saw and Torvald didn't seem to care at all. The noise in the room was getting high.

"Guys, keep it down. Someone might hear us." I walked over to the door and peeked down the stairs.

"Lina's right. We should leave." Yusef deleted our last locations. I crept down to the ped-way and peered out the glass onto the darkened courtyard. The lampposts that lined the sidewalks usually stayed lit all night, but tonight they were as black as the sky. Hardly any of the dorm lights were on either. I couldn't see anything. My guts started churning. Something was very wrong.

"Guys," I whispered up the stairs.

They were about to come stomping down when I raised my hand, fingers spread wide. Jan's eyes met mine and I could see she felt what I felt. Fear.

Small drops of precipitation were sliding down the outside of the glass, distorting our view of the night. The darkness was like a thick vapour, alive and breathing against the glass. We waited in stillness amid pounding hearts. Jan put her hand on my shoulder, trying to read my mind. I shook my head. My eyes strained through the dark, making out the shadows of buildings, the pathway—something moved. Jan saw it too.

She pulled me backward into the fitness centre and we glided down the stairs toward the pool. It was a good thing we had so much practice at being sneaky. Nobody made a peep. Yusef waved us to the north door, away from the dorms. He opened the locks and let in the night air. It was cold enough we could see our breath. That's what I had seen. A fog of breath. We all broke into a run, crouching over the frosted grass, heading for the shelter of the trees.

Getting caught out of our dorms was one thing, but this felt almost life threatening. We had stumbled across some government secret that would eliminate any form of resistance in order to remain protected. We were that resistance and we were in over our heads. We just hit the trees when we heard the north door to the pool slam shut. Torvald gave the signal to split up, fingers flat then opening out. We silently obeyed, except for Glynis of course. Yusef ran off campus, Jan ran toward the law buildings and I stealthily manoeuvred round about toward the dorms again. We would all meet back at the girls dorms as we had in the past.

I breathed into my sleeve so my foggy breath wouldn't give me away. I slid from one tree to another, making sure the shuffling noise I heard went past me. I caught a glimpse of them at one point. It appeared to be some sort of cult. Four figures, all wearing black cloaks, with hooded faces and hidden hands. They must have been professors—old ones—because they were too bulgy and slow to be students. I stayed in the shadows and let them pass. As soon as they were out of earshot, I bolted for the dorms.

When I got to my room, I was the only one there. I had taken the most risky but shortest route back, so I wasn't surprised. First thing I did was call my parents.

A groggy voice answered and I winced, knowing I had woken them up. As I spat out my story, I threw on my backpack. I was getting out of here.

"Halina? What on earth are you calling for? It's one-thirty."

"Sorry, Mom, it's an emergency. Remember what you said about Spencer? He isn't the only student who has disappeared. There are more—" I stopped. Someone was walking down the hallway. Thank goodness, someone else made it back. The doorknob turned...

"Halina, what are you saying? Is it not safe for you? Halina?" I could hear my mom's voice in the receiver, even though I had pulled the phone away from my ear and dropped it on the bed. The person at the door was not one of my friends. It was a man in a long black cloak. It was Principal Arter.

I backed up until my legs hit the side of my bed. The open window behind me was my only escape. If I could only get around the bed before—

"Miss Pawlak. It seems you're in a heap of trouble, young lady." Arter's jowls shook. His huge lips protruded over long teeth, his hands hidden in his cloak. He could be holding anything under there, pointing anything at me. "Where are the others—Mr. Hassam, Mr. Peters, Miss Kurauchi and Miss Thatcher?"

"I don't know." I sidestepped the foot of the bed, and then froze as three more hooded figures blocked the door. An unknown voice rose from beneath a hood, "We have secured Miss Kurauchi."

"Excellent."

No. Not Jan. I tried to keep my composure. Then I remembered the plug in my pocket. The plug I wasn't supposed to use except in an emergency. I'd told my mom this was an emergency. My mom. Was she still on the line?

The principal grabbed my arm, so I started yelling. "Mom! They're kidnapping me. Send help!"

Arter's eyes bugged out and he released me to dash to the phone. He snatched it off the bed to hang it up.

This was my chance.

I plunged backward, grabbing the edge of the windowsill. I shoved my head through the opening and came face to face with Yusef as he was climbing up the trellis. I almost kissed him, he was so close. He must have heard the voices in my room. He knew the trouble I was in and silently mouthed my name.

I shook my head warning him to remain quiet. I could have made it out if he hadn't stalled me. Hands grabbed my legs, pulling me backward. I strained to keep hold of the ledge. Yusef grabbed my arms trying to pull me toward him.

"No," I shouted, looking into his fearful eyes. I wasn't going to let him get caught too. Someone had to escape to tell our parents—to put a stop to this. Yusef squeezed his eyes shut, but he did not let go. I was being ripped in half.

"Miss Pawlak." Arter was growling. "Let go immediately."

Yusef remained quietly struggling. He looked desperate to help me.

"Let go." I winced, directing my comment at both ends of my body.

Yusef's footing on the trellis was slipping. He lost his grip and fell to the ground. My hold on the windowsill tore at the muscles in my fingers until I had to let go. They dragged me by my legs onto the floor.

"What's your problem?" I yelled, rubbing my legs where hand-shaped bruises formed. If I could keep their attention on me, Yusef might have a chance to escape.

Arter's face was invading my space. "You are going to regret your actions tonight." His droopy mouth sprayed spit on me.

"Well, so are you," I sprayed back.

He slapped my face.

I gasped.

"Get her up," he growled. Another hooded man grabbed my shoulders and hauled me to my feet. They rifled through my pack, looking for who knows what. They let me keep it, but Arter confiscated my phone.

"Let's go." They escorted me out the door. One of them peered out the window, but Yusef had already run out of sight.

As we stepped out into the chilly night air, I searched for any sign of my friends. I found Yusef spying around the corner of the building.

He must still be determined to free me.

I sized up the four hooded men and knew Yusef couldn't beat them. When my captor bumped beside me, I could feel the handle of a gun under his cloak. It was too risky for Yusef to try anything. The plug was the only choice I had left. It was the only way.

With all my strength I yanked free of my captor's grasp and ran in the opposite direction of Yusef. I only had seconds before they caught up to me.

"Get back here."

I heard the safety click off the gun, but I didn't look back. I reached into my pocket and ripped out the plug. A shot fired, singeing a lock of my hair. Gasping, I brought the plug up to my neck and touched it to the imprint.

Everything went dark.

Chapter 6

I awoke to the buzzing of my alarm clock. I was lying in my dorm room bed. Jan was in the bed beside me, mashing a pillow over her head. It was 7:00 am. I bolted upright.

"What happened? How long have I been sleeping?"

"Argh, stop yelling." Jan's voice came out from under the pillow. I leapt over to her, shaking her hard.

"How did you get here? How did I get here?"

"Stop shaking me." She threw the pillow in my face. "You must have had a nightmare."

A nightmare? No, it was real. It had to be. But Jan had been caught. I had been caught. "What did we do last night?" I was in my pink pyjamas. As I changed, I noticed the bruises on my arms and legs. My phone was sitting on my desk. How did it get there? I picked it up to check for messages. There were none. What?

Jan already had her nose in a book. "Studied. We have a Logic exam on Friday."

"You don't remember sneaking out to hack into RAS?"

She looked up. "I don't sneak out. Hey, where did you get those bruises? And what is RAS?"

"I got them when Principal Arter hauled me through a window. RAS is the mainframe for this school's criminal security system and you do sneak out—all the time. You see this?" I grabbed the chopped-off lock of hair. "This happened when a bullet whizzed past my head."

Maybe they zapped her brain. Maybe they erased her memory. If that were the case, then how come I could remember? It must be because of the plug. Where was it? I checked my pockets. I checked the floor. I rummaged through my bed sheets and found it beside my pillow.

"Recognize this?" I shoved the plug up to her face. She shook her head. "Come on, Jan, I need you to remember. I need to know what happened to you."

"You are going psycho," she stated.

"These plugs are like portals into some new reality. I must have shifted when I touched it to my imprint."

"Whoa. When did you get that silver tattoo?"

"We all have one."

"Who are *we*? Because I would never get a tattoo." She lifted up her black hair and showed me her smooth, tattoo-less neck. "And the principal's name is Nelsen." She got up and locked herself in the bathroom.

I did sound a bit psychotic.

I looked at the plug and read the number, 346181 with the words *Safe Place* etched on the side. Jan's memory wasn't erased. This was a completely different Jan. This was a completely different reality.

I sped across the hall and burst into Glynis's room.

"Hey. Do you mind?" A black girl was standing by the window brushing her teeth. I didn't know who she was, but she wasn't Glynis or Paula.

"Where's Glynis Thatcher?"

"Honey, I don't know who you talkin' 'bout, but there ain't no Glynis livin' in this room."

"What about Paula?"

"Nu-uh. You got the wrong room, girl."

"Oh. Sorry for barging in on you."

I closed the door. I ran down the hall to the stairway window. I could see the ped-way across the courtyard, but the attic space above it didn't exist. No secret room. No RAS. No girly message to say *Halina Pawlak: Status: Shifter.*

I had to find out what was going on. Yusef would know. I knew he would be in the computer lab, so I skipped my first class and went to find him. The lab was packed with early-morning students trying to finish their various assignments. The first person I noticed was Spencer Wright. A wave of relief flooded over me. He was fine. He wasn't even expelled.

"Spencer. Hey, are you okay?" I went up and hugged him.

"Hey, Lina, wassup?" He pointed his gun fingers at me. His big, infectious smile lit up his face.

"Well..." I paused. This version of Spencer probably didn't even know about his own traumatic experience. I couldn't even tell him. I stumbled my way through a superficial cover-up. "I just wanted to check up on you, see how you were doing." I stifled my feelings, knowing he would be utterly confused if I got all emotional. Luckily, he didn't notice.

"Same old. Loaded with homework and no time to finish it. Hey, you don't usually have a spare now. Are you skipping again?"

"Ha, you know me." My eyes evaded his and wandered across the room. I spotted Yusef. I freed myself from my current conversation. "I'll catch ya later, Spence."

"Yeah, catch ya." Spencer immediately had another conversation going with other friends.

I threw my backpack to the floor beside Yusef and hugged him.

"What are you doing?" he asked, eyes widening in surprise.

"Sorry, I can't explain, I'm just glad to see you." I sat down beside him and, ust to be sure, I glanced at his neck. No imprint. Nobody had one except me.

"Um, can you remind me what your name is again?" he asked with a look of bewilderment.

I stared at him, wondering what sort of game he was playing. "Halina."

"Oh, right. Sorry, I forgot. So, Halina, what do you want?"

I swallowed hard. "You always call me Lina." My hands shook. What had happened to my best friends? It was starting to scare me.

"Halina, I haven't talked to you since grade seven. I have homework to do, so what do you want?"

This was a nightmare, just like Jan had said. A nightmare that was real. "Nothing, I guess. Sorry to bug you. No, wait. Do you know where the school's main computer is?"

"Yeah, it's in Nelsen's office, of course." He turned back to his screen.

"Thanks. Sorry for bugging you." I touched his hand before I left. As I walked away, I saw him look at his hand, then look at me and smile.

I walked out to the courtyard and slumped onto a concrete bench. A cold breeze rustled the leaves in the trees. The sound reminded me that another Alberta winter was on its way. I shivered. Could I really stay in this place when Jan was so weird, Glynis was nowhere to be found and Yusef hardly knew who I was? At least Spencer was okay. Still, I felt trapped. I had to find a way out of here.

A group of noisy, obnoxious boys were across the courtyard laughing and teasing each other. I realized one of them was Torvald, so I ran over.

"Hey, Tor."

He turned to me. "Do I know you?" He looked down on me, his

friends snickering behind him.

"Yeah, it's Halina. Uh, you used to date a friend of mine. Could I talk to you for a minute?" By this time, it didn't surprise me that he didn't know me. Everything had changed except me. His friends snickered louder as we walked away.

"So I was wondering if you could help me out with something." I shoved my hands in my pockets, trying to avoid exposing them to the frigid air. The plug was in there and I gripped it tightly.

"I don't think so, but hit me with it." He was tall, especially when he stared down to me.

"I need you to get us sent to the principal's office."

He chuckled. "Why would I do that?"

"I need to see Ar—Nelsen's computer."

"Listen, hon, I've been in that office plenty. What do you need to know about her 'puter?"

"Is it big? Like a screen with blue plasma that flows down it? Are there these glass tubes filled with black plugs that look like this?" I held up the plug.

"What pills you been popping?" He stopped walking and glared at me. "Are you mad? It's a Mac. A pink one. It's butt-ugly and it crashes on her all the time. Now, if you came here to ask me out, hurry up. I'm busy." He folded his muscular arms across his muscular chest and stared down at me again.

I rolled my eyes. He never treated me this way. "Out of respect for Glynis, I'll pretend you didn't say that."

I walked away as he said, "Who's Glynis?"

If I had this figured out right, Coach Tyler shifted here on his days off. If I saw him yesterday, back in that...old place—whatever I should call it—then he should be here today in this *new* place.

Bursting through the doors to the pool, I saw him right away, gorgeous, as always. He focused on me, blue eyes peering into my soul as if he was trying to read my thoughts.

"Mr. Tyler? Can I speak with you?" When I approached him, he put his arms on my shoulders. His hands were warm.

"Miss Pawlak, training is about to start."

"I know, but I need to talk to you about what happened."

"Last night?"

I nodded. He knew. What a relief.

"You need to go change. You have training."

Other students were coming in and out of the change room. We couldn't talk right now, so I went to my locker. At least he knew. At last someone could explain this whole thing.

During practice, he kept his eyes on me. He was watching me as if I was going to disappear right in front of him. I pushed myself to race through a couple of laps. After the front stroke, I flipped to my back. I watched the ceiling markers as they swiftly went by. When I started to tire, coach would give his favourite bit of encouragement. Keep going. Anything for him. All of this extra training had really increased my speed. I considered myself officially whipped into shape.

I waited until everyone else had left. When I got to the edge of the pool, Coach Tyler's face loomed over me.

"So this is where you go on your days off." I sat on the edge of the pool with a towel wrapped around me.

"I'm keeping my options open." He sat down beside me, leaning his arm on his knee. "Now I've given those options to you. You have merged with your alternate self. Now you are one person. Your alternate has a whole life full of different memories. The longer you stay here, the more you will regain those memories."

"So if I leave this reality, there won't be an alternate me to fill in the gap? I'll just disappear?"

"You'll go missing. It's a side effect of shifting realities. But why would you leave? You don't ever need to. The Special Force doesn't exist in this reality, so you are safe. That's why I call this one *Safe Place*. You could call them by their plug number, but I prefer giving them names. Your home reality, I call *Big Brother*."

I stared at him. As tempting as it was to be this close, I felt that he was wrong. I would want to go back.

"What about Glynis, where is she?"

"She doesn't exist here."

That wouldn't do. I had to fix it. "What if she shifted here?"

"You can't force something to exist in another reality. She would appear, though she wouldn't be registered at school and people wouldn't know her. She would be a stranger to everyone but you and me." He stared me down again, holding his chin while running a finger across his lips.

I tried hard not to get distracted by the movement. This shifting business gave me a good reason to have a one-on-one conversation with him, but I had to pay attention to what he was telling me. I snapped out of my daze and tried to listen.

"There are times when certain objects do not fit into the reality. That object would automatically take the form of something that fit here."

"Like what?"

"If you create something, like a homework assignment, then try to shift with it. It will appear as a blank piece of paper. The paper exists, but your creation doesn't. You would have to rewrite it."

He was filling my mind with unfathomable things, verbal and non-verbal. I was trying to wrap my head around this metaphysical knowledge while my heart was dealing with the close proximity of Coach Tyler's body.

"Do you think you'll be okay?" he asked.

"Okay with what?"

"With staying here in Safe Place."

"With my friends all back there in Big Brother Regime-land getting caught and punished, maybe even killed? I don't think so." I snapped out of Gerome-Tyler heaven and remembered the fear I had felt last night.

"Yes, except here they are all fine."

"They are *not* fine. They are all weird. And Glynis, what about her?"

"You can't save everyone's alternate in every reality. That is impossible. You could go back to get her, but that would only get you killed. Safe Place may have a few differences, but it is by far the better choice. Lina, you just have to cut your losses."

He never called me Lina. A glint of something new flashed in his eyes. He leaned closer. "And besides," he said, displaying his brilliant, dimpled smile, "in this reality you and I are together." In case I didn't catch his drift, he bent his head down and kissed me. It was a long-imagined kiss. I pushed my lips against his and combed my fingers into his perfect hair. It was bliss. It was euphoric. It was everything.

It left me speechless. My lips tingled in aftershock. He could see my shock and chuckled. "Acting professional and distant with you in Reality Big Brother was quite amusing." He helped me to my feet. "No extra practice today, the pool is getting drained." Noticing his complete recovery from the kiss begged a question. "Coach Tyler, that wasn't our first kiss, was it?"

"No, it wasn't." His dimples appeared again. "Give it a few more hours, you'll remember. And in private, you call me Gerome."

Chapter 7

I sat at my dorm room desk pinching the bridge of my nose, trying to decide how I felt—ecstatic and full of dread, mixed together with a bit of disappointment. I actually made it to classes, but none of my teachers were the same. No Professor Petersen and no String Theory assignment. No one had imprints and there were no security doors to clock my attendance.

Torvald laughed at me when I passed him in the hall. Could I live with this? In a place where I didn't belong? I could shift again, but any other world would be just as weird—or worse. Was Reality Big Brother so dangerous that I could never go back?

Within that same thought, I could feel my heart race, remembering Coach Tyler. *Gerome*. We were together. I wanted to squeal like the little school girl I was. Dating my swim coach was such a dream.

"Hey, you okay?" It was Jan. "I hope you're not worried about the exam on Friday. You'll do great."

Her face was back in a book before I could think of something to tell her. The last two days had thrown a bucket-load of stress in my face. Some of my long-term memories were warping and changing. The major life-changing decisions were the same, but the details were changing. Like the fact that Glynis wasn't in any of them. I was afraid I would forget her completely. I looked at Jan—my only friend who supposedly knew me. I didn't understand her new straightedge ways. I couldn't blame her for not seeing my dilemma. How could anyone?

"I'm going to do some laps at the pool." Maybe it would calm me down.

"Coach Tyler doesn't work today."

"No, really, I'm just going to swim."

She picked up on my comment. "Really? I thought you were motivated more by a passion for your coach, not a passion for the sport."

"Yeah, well, not this time."

"Know what? I'll come with you. Could you use the company?"

"Yeah."

It was good to know this strange version of Jan was still my best friend.

As we walked, I started to feel lightheaded. Images of my past started flashing through my mind. I tried to blink them out of my head, but they blinded me. They were memories I hadn't had. Memories of hanging out with my friends, except Glynis wasn't among them. I stopped.

"What's up?" Jan asked.

"I don't know..." I watched my life like it was a movie. The memories were real. They were a part of me. "Do you remember riding the bus home from middle school?" I could hear the clunky engine gearing down at every stop. I could smell sweet peas and the ocean, even though I knew I wasn't back at home in Victoria.

"Yeah."

"Where was Glynis? I'm sure she was with us."

"Who is Glynis?"

I shook my head. I would never get used to this. I forced myself to remember a time when we'd been with Glynis. I remembered the rave during the heat of summer...

"Come on, Jan, don't be so scared." Glynis was trying to convince her it was all right to sneak in without paying. *"What's the worst that could happen? We get kicked out. Nothing new."*

"Besides," I said, *"I'm not going to miss The Consonant C. They are the best indie-tronica on earth."*

We were standing in the parking lot waiting for Yusef's brother, Ibram, to come out.

"You better not jump out, or you'll make Jan pee her pants." Yusef yelled, seemingly to no one.

Ibram came out from behind a parked car, laughing. *"How did you know I was there?"*

Yusef snickered. *"Years of practice."*

They laughed and punched each other.

Ibram handed us his friends' tickets. *"Everyone else is already inside. Give these back when you get in."*

We approached the door, fake IDs in hand. The ambient music

pulsed from inside.

The memory started to fade. I tried to focus on it and remember what happened next, but it disappeared as if someone had pushed a stop button.

I looked at Jan. "That's why you're so uptight. You never had Glynis to encourage you. She was our momentum. She convinced you to sneak into the rave last—"

"Rave? We never went to a rave."

I couldn't get through to her. Not this way.

We walked the rest of the way in silence.

When we got to the pool, it was empty, drained. Oh yeah. We stood there for a moment, gazing at the bottom of the pool.

I released a quiet groan. My confusion scrambled my sense of purpose like an omelette. I felt defeated from a battle I hadn't yet fought.

As I wallowed in my self-pity, I stared absently at the walls of the pool. It was strange how different they looked when they weren't underwater. Very strange. I saw a pattern in the blue and white tiles that I hadn't noticed before. Simple rectangles that reminded me of the ones framing the secret door. I walked down into the bottom of the pool to get a closer look.

"Lina? What are you doing?" I jumped at Jan's voice.

"I'll be there in a sec. Why don't you go save us a seat in the cafeteria? It's almost supper." I dragged my hand along the tiles.

"What's that?" she asked.

I looked up and noticed she was pointing at something. I followed her finger. She came down the slanted floor of the pool and touched the tile before I saw it. It wasn't a tile at all. It was made of rubber. A square blue button made to look like a tile. I felt alarmed—just like the time Jan found the secret room.

"Go up top and tell me what happens when I push this."

She obeyed. I pressed it. I heard a soft thump that matched the thumping in my chest.

"Oh, wow," she said.

I ran up the slanted floor and up the steps. Again, Jan pointed and I followed her gaze. A window revealed Coach Tyler's office. On the far side, a row of lockers jutted out from the wall on a hinge. Behind the locker door, a faint blue glow emanated from inside.

I gasped. "Another secret room." I took a step forward.

"Wait!" Jan grabbed my arm. "I think we should leave. We have an exam tomorrow. We should go eat, then go back to our dorms and stay there and study."

I turned to her. "Jan, you're not like this. You have a spirit of adventure. You have courage. I've seen it. Come on, this is important."

"We are not supposed to go into teacher's offices, especially ones with secret rooms."

I grabbed her arm. "This is my boyfriend's office. I'm sure *I've* been in here before."

The door to the office, surprisingly, was not locked. We crept in and pushed the lockers out of the way. It was déjà vu in a major way. Coach Tyler's version of the Real Administration System was smaller, cruder, with no fancy graphics or glass tubes. The plugs were stored in a cardboard box. I tried to explain it all to Jan, but I didn't know what she would understand, so I tried to show her. I dropped my backpack and sat down in front of the computer. To my utter relief, no sickly-sweet audio response came out. I tried to find student files. No file existed for them, so I found the Shifters.

"See? There's me. Halina Pawlak. Status, Shifter. Location, 346181."

Jan didn't say anything, so I went on, "And there is Gerome Tyler. He shifts to 346181 on his days off."

"But Lina, his location says that's where he is now." Jan pointed to the numbers 346181.

"Oh, crap. We have to get out of here."

"Wait. I believe you. You need to give me one of those tattoos."

"What?" I turned, startled by her sudden conversion. "I don't know how."

"Well, figure it out. Fast."

I typed "identification imprints" into the search bar. My fingers weren't working and I fumbled to delete a few typos. Nothing came up. I tried "apply barcode" and still nothing.

"I c-can't," I stuttered. "There's no equipment. I need a syringe with this gel stuff. It gets injected into you somehow. I wasn't even looking when they did it to me."

Jan was pawing through the junk on the desk. "There are no syringes or anything." Her voice was full of panic. "What do I do?"

I stopped and scrunched up my eyes, pinching the bridge of my nose. Think, think. When I came here, I kept my imprint even though I merged with an alternate that didn't have one. That was it.

"Your other self has an imprint. If she shifts here, she will merge with you. You'll keep the imprint."

"Well, can you go and get her?"

"I can't. She's been captured. I don't know where she is."

"What?"

A sudden noise shocked us both as a door closed out in the pool area. Jan brought a hand over her mouth. We couldn't get caught in here. I peered from behind the door made of lockers and into Gerome's office. I looked through the windows, out to the pool, but didn't see anyone.

"Quick, let's get out of here."

"Wait, you should take these with you." She pointed to the box full of plugs.

"Yeah. Good idea." I carefully tipped the box into my backpack, cringing at the clunking noise. Standing back up, I entered the office once again, in time to see Gerome staring at me through the glass. My heart burst like a cannon. Sweat covered my skin. He hadn't seen Jan yet, so I closed the door of lockers and hid her inside. I just hoped she would take the hint and not try to come out.

"Lina?" He approached the door. "What are you doing in here?" He looked in my eyes, and sudden flashes of unknown memories blocked my vision. Memories of us texting each other, meeting at a cafe down the street, holding hands across the table...I shook my head trying to focus.

"Why do you have an RAS computer hidden in your office?" I countered.

He halted. "They've found you. They will be here any minute."

"What? How?" The extra weight of the plugs was like a pile of rocks in my backpack. Would he notice?

"The detection door to my office. Didn't you see it?" I looked up, and sure enough, a thin, metal strip crossed the doorjamb. That metal strip had been on the top of every single door of the school in 047829. I kicked myself for not noticing it.

"I thought you said there weren't any. You said the Special Force doesn't exist here."

He approached me cautiously and clasped his hands to my arms. "There's only this one—to keep tabs on me."

"You lied to me," I accused. "You exist here. You are a judge for the Over-Ride Project. You are Special Force. You brought me to Safe Place to prevent me from opposing it. You took the plug for Big Brother so I could never get back. You thought I would just settle right in and forget all about the tyrannical oppression ruining my world as we speak. Have you done anything to stop it, or do you even want it stopped?"

"Nobody can stop it. But we can escape it. I'll grab you another plug. Send you away for a while, and when it's safe—"

"No." I blocked him from moving closer to the hidden room. I couldn't let him discover Jan. Plus, he would find out I had stolen all the plugs. "Why have there been people going missing?" I rerouted, trying to sound strong, even though I was shaking inside.

He turned to me. "They're classified undesirable. They don't qualify."

"Don't qualify for what?"

"To be members of Special Force—to be candidates for Over-Ride. They are using Big Brother, and a few other realities, to create a superior army. It has nothing to do with race, or religion, or station—this is about all humans. Corrupt DNA has been allowed to integrate and mingle with ours for generations. Humans have abandoned the concept of survival of the fittest and allowed even the weak to survive. Where nature would have weeded them out a long time ago, we build hospitals and social programs that allow them to live and procreate—to pass on their sicknesses and deformities until our species is a watered down image of non-perfection. We will never be able to reach our full potential if they are allowed to live among us."

I was shocked at the things coming out of his mouth. "So you have them murdered?"

"No. Come on, Over-Ride is not some annihilation project or communist regime. We just send them away. That's why I was trying to work you so hard on the swim team. I was giving you extra training to increase your fitness level so you would qualify as a candidate."

"I knew I was not the best on the swim team. You lied to me about your motives."

He took me in his arms and kissed the top of my head. It was impossible for me to pull away.

"Being chosen for Over-Ride is a great honour. I didn't want to lose you. I didn't want you to be sent away."

His desperate tone made me melt. Why? Why did he have to act so caring and sensitive while simultaneously divulging all of this horrible information?

"You would have left me here." I stepped back, separating myself from the warmth of his body. I took my accusation one step further, hoping I was wrong. "You don't care about me. You were just abusing my feelings for you so I wouldn't find out who you really are." I wanted so badly to be wrong. I studied his face for a sign.

His expression turned cold and his response cut deep. "You should have listened to me, but you are so stubborn. I gave you what you wanted, but it wasn't enough."

This man with the face of an angel had something seriously wrong with him. My heart broke. I couldn't have him. Not like this.

"Where do you send them? The people who don't reach the bar?"

"Some other reality where they can live their lives like nothing is wrong with them."

"Have you been there?"

"Of course not. Once you go there you can't come back."

Something moved in my peripheral vision. Out the office window, I could see dark figures entering the pool area. They were wearing dark, hooded cloaks like devilish spectres. How ridiculous. I turned back to Gerome.

"That's right. You would never stoop so low. You would never be caught mingling with the commoners. You wouldn't even date me until I reached your level of expectation." I backed up.

"It's my job to judge you."

"Yeah, just like Principal Arter did to me and all my friends." I slowly lowered my backpack until I reached the zipper. I slid it up just enough to get my hand inside. "If you thought I would just hang out here for the rest of my life and pretend nothing was wrong, then you don't know me. I'm no coward." The hooded figures were approaching the office. My fingers grabbed the first plug I could reach. "If you were a good boyfriend, you would know me better than that."

"Lina, what are you doing?"

He tried to lunge for me, but I was faster. I whipped my hand up and touched the plug to my neck before he could stop me.

Chapter 8

The air was cold, with a strong wind. I opened my eyes and looked across a rolling field of barley, lined with clumps of trees. The pool was gone. All the buildings were gone except a small farmhouse tucked between a wooden granary and a red-roofed barn. It reminded me of a scene out of *Little House on the Prairie*.

Once I realized I was safe and alone, I began to cry. My relationship with Gerome was fake. I felt like a victim and a fool. I thought I knew what I was doing. I thought I was worthy of his affection, but I was being singled out as a troublemaker. Again. Life was so unfair.

I must have been displaced a great distance because this was nowhere near the city. Everything felt wrong. I looked around. I saw the North Saskatchewan River in the distance, positioned exactly how it would be if winding through the city. Except the city wasn't there.

In its place stood a small fort on the north bank. Fort Edmonton. Just like the replicated tourist attraction I had visited during a school field trip. I remembered all of the employees were in period costumes.

Looking down, I saw I was wearing one of those same costumes—a long dress and white apron. I had a pioneer bonnet on my head. My backpack was gone, replaced with a kerchief tied to a stick. I picked it up and checked to make sure the plugs were still inside. What the heck? Had I gone back in time? I didn't think that was possible.

I thought of shifting again, but where would that get me? Since I was here, it wouldn't hurt to look around.

A horse-drawn cart was tottering across the field from the direction of the farm. A man and wife sat up front looking just like Mr. and Mrs. Ingalls. The rickety wheels were bumping along in two muddy ruts. I dried my eyes as they approached.

"Hello, stranger." The man pulled on the reins and tipped his hat. "Would you like a lift into town?"

"Um, sure. I mean yes, thank you."

"Hop in the back then."

I walked around to the back of the cart and took a breath. Four children snuggled under a blanket between crates of live chickens. Okay. I could handle this. I found a space just big enough for my butt and dangled my legs over the edge. The children's gaze drilled into me.

"Hey, can you tell me what year it is?" I asked.

They looked at each other and then back to me. The oldest spoke up. "Its twenty-twelve—at least for a couple months, still." His answer didn't explain anything about the situation.

"Oh, right. Of course." I felt stupid.

So, if I hadn't time traveled...then this must be the way it was in this reality. I took a discreet look at the plug I had used. Over the numbers was the words *Wild West* in Gerome's handwriting. That was for sure. I sat quietly as the cart bumped over the uneven ground. Was Jan in trouble? They probably found her by now, and I couldn't do anything about it.

It took a painfully long time to get to the fort. Every bump in the meagre road added another bruise to my butt. Then we had to ferry across the river where the Low Level Bridge should have been. It took an hour. They shared their supper, which consisted of baked beans and bread. By the time we reached the town-site, it was dark.

"You've got a place to stay then?" the mother asked.

"Well, no, not really."

"Have you got any money? There's a hotel in town."

"No, I haven't."

"Well, I can allow you to stay in the stable for now." She pointed where the father was leading the horses around the side the house. She handed me the wool blanket that the kids had been using in the back of the cart. It was extremely heavy and smelled like the excrement of chickens. *Okay*, I thought again, *I can handle this.*

I cautiously checked the lintel of the door for a security bar before I walked through. I wondered how long I should stay here. I had to come up with a plan. I stacked up a pile of hay and laid the blanket on top of it. I assessed the situation. It seemed that whatever I was touching at the time I shifted came with me, however altered. Remembering the contents of my backpack when I shifted, I dumped the kerchief onto the floor to get a look. First, my swimming suit and towel fell out, altered the same way as my clothes. The result was not pretty. My wallet was old-fashioned too. My iPod was a diner bell and my cell phone had turned into a horseshoe. Only the plugs remained the same.

I thought about where I would reappear if I shifted back to my reality. If I had an alternate self, I would have ended up exactly where they were, merging instantly. But what if there was no alternate me? I had appeared in the middle of a field. Did that mean the field was the same global position as Gerome's office? I assumed so. So where did I want to be standing when I shifted?

I sifted through the plugs, looking for one I recognized. What was it? 041—no—047 something. I hoped I'd remember. Then I found it. 047829. Big Brother.

Sighing with relief, I wrapped the kerchief back together and put the plug in my apron pocket. Tomorrow I was going to go home, find everyone and save them—without getting caught. The question was *how*?

One of the pioneer children kicked my leg, waking me up. As soon as I moved, the child ran away. She had placed a bowl of steaming, grey mush beside me...*yum*. I ate it until my mouth dried out so much that I gagged. It was time to stop mooching off this nice family. I left the stable. Their property was just outside the barricade to the fort.

The doors were open and unguarded, so I entered. The courtyard of the fort was loud and muddy. Above all, it smelled awful. Everywhere I looked, horses were stepping in their own feces. People stepped in it too.

I jumped up onto a boardwalk to avoid it, but there was horse feces up there too. Hundreds of footprints made of fecal matter. Gross. I blinked my eyes rapidly to stop them from watering.

It could be worse. Don't make such a big deal. To these people, this is completely normal. Memorize the number of this reality.

I didn't want to come here too often.

The boardwalk led to a trading post, blacksmith, milliner, baker, carpenter, and a barber. Men with frizzy beards chewing tobacco sat outside a saloon, hats over their eyes. Women in floor-length skirts, holding babies and baskets, scolded the vagrants as they walked by.

For a brief moment, I thought it might be a movie set. I looked around for hidden cameras, but realized a movie set wouldn't smell like an outhouse. I poked my head into the trading post. The cashier stood behind a barred window, talking with the customer at the front of a long line. I took a spot at the back and waited my turn. What I had to find was some kind of tool or weapon I could use to rescue my friends. Some way to get past the detection gates. Some help. How was I going to pay for anything? Maybe I could work in compensation.

As I stood there, I noticed a small square cut out of the wall up by the ceiling. The barrel of a rifle was conspicuously at the ready, aiming at the customers. At first, I thought I should yell and duck. Then I realized it was like a Wild West version of a security camera.

When it was my turn, I approached the man behind the bars. "What are the bars for?"

He spat toward a spittoon and missed. "Keep the Injuns out."

"Oh. Um, I was wondering if you needed some help. I'd like to work off the price of a gun."

"Don't need a hand. Already got one."

"Oh. Do you know where I could get a job?"

"Yeah, second floor of the hotel." He pointed across the street to the balcony of the hotel, where two ladies laughed with each other, wearing nothing but lacy underwear. The men outside the saloon were whistling. No wonder they sat there all day.

"Very funny."

The cashier gave me a grin. His front teeth were missing. "You new in town?"

"I guess you could call it that."

"Someone was looking for you." He grinned again.

"What?" I yelled, making everyone in the line behind me jump. "Were they wearing black cloaks?" My heart thumped hard.

"Naw, it was my *Injun* that works in the back."

I took a deep breath. "I thought these bars were supposed to keep Indians out."

"Hey, Injun." The loud call made everyone jump again.

The back door opened, revealing a young man in grey trousers and suspenders over a dirty, white shirt. He was carrying a sack of flour in front of his face. As he dropped it to the ground, I squealed in shock.

"Yusef!"

"Lina."

He tried to run up to the counter, but the cashier thumped him on the head.

"There ain't no approaching the counter, Injun. Go 'round back."

"Yes, sir." He ran out the door.

"You better go get him. He ain't allowed in the front."

I blinked. "Oh." I darted away. As soon as I turned the corner, Yusef grabbed me in a hug that picked me up off the ground.

"I am so glad to see you," he exploded.

"You better stop it." My cheek squished against his chest. "Let go before someone sees you."

He released me. "These nut-jobs think I'm an Indian."

"Yusef, you *are* an Indian."

"No, like Native American Indian. I'm not allowed in any of the shops. I only got a job because I promised to hide my face, and I have to sleep under the stairs."

"I slept in a barn last night."

"How did you get here?"

I showed him my hobo-stick full of plugs. "I stole them from Gerome. He had a whole stash."

"Is that horseshoe your cell phone?"

"Yeah, how did you know?"

"Mine did the same thing."

"Hey, how did you get here?"

Yusef sat down on an empty barrel. "That night you disappeared, Arter was enraged. He stomped around on the grass throwing a temper tantrum. He yelled at everyone. 'Who gave her that plug? Who is the traitor? If you don't get her back, I'm going to...blah, blah, blah.'"

"What happened then?"

"They all went back to RAS and began assigning themselves different realities to search and look for you. Apparently, they can't find what reality you're in until you go through a detection gate and I haven't seen any here. I don't think they have RAS in this reality. Anyways, I followed them. They began disappearing just like you did. At the last moment, I reached out and touched Arter right as he disappeared. Even if he saw me, he had no time to react because everything changed. All of the sudden we were dressed like this in the saloon, sitting at a table covered in empty whiskey glasses. He might have recognized me, but he was suddenly slobbering drunk. He just passed out. As soon as other people saw me, they booted me outside. They said Injuns weren't allowed. I haven't seen him since."

"I know what happened," I said. "He had an alternate that he merged with. If his alternate was drunk, then he instantly became drunk. No wonder he passed out. How come Arter has an alternate here, but not us?"

"Who knows, it could have happened a million different ways. Maybe our parents died. Maybe they never even got married. Every reality has its own story."

"So why does everything look four-hundred years old?"

"Apparently, the dark ages in Europe lasted a lot longer. North America wasn't settled till centuries later."

"That sounds stupid."

"Glynis would know how history's progress could have halted, especially if it lacked a couple of influential people."

"Like the guy who invented the printing press," I said.

"Or the guy who said the world was round. Any number of little decisions could radically alter history."

We fell into silence, realizing the depth of the situation we were in. I noticed Yusef staring at me and it made me *really* uncomfortable.

"Lina, you look good." His warm eyes smiled.

Was he flirting with me?

"You look...ridiculous."

To prove my point, he snapped his hokey suspenders and clicked his heels. We both laughed.

It was easier to laugh and feign ignorance than contemplate another plunge into hormone-hell. My heart was still in upheaval from my two-day rollercoaster with Gerome—so much work gone to waste so fast. I had to get this all sorted out. Then maybe...

"So what now?" he asked.

I refocused. "You can help me."

"With what?"

"With finding Jan, Glynis and Torvald and getting them out of Big Brother."

He blanched. "You're gonna what? That is impossible. Back home there are detection gates on every door. There are Special Force pawns everywhere. You'll get caught."

"The doors are monitored, but not the windows." I smiled. "Come on, Yusef. I need you."

Was I flirting too? So much for feigning ignorance. I was such a hypocrite.

He looked doubtful, so I encouraged him. "I got out of there. You got out. We can't just leave them."

"Well, where would we go? We're not coming back here. I'm not going to be someone's lackey for the rest of my life."

"I've got about a hundred of these," I said, picking up some plugs and dropping them back into the kerchief. "We'll just try them all until we find one that we like."

He pursed his lips. "Okay. You've convinced me. Let's go."

As we stepped out of the alley, I knew something was wrong. I heard a woman scream and a pane of glass smash. Then I saw them. Six men in cloaks, riding black horses. They were all holding guns. They were Special Force and they were looking for me.

The leader yelled, "There is a stranger hiding in this town and I want her found. She's got red hair and brown eyes. I want her brought out, or I'm gonna burn down this fort with all you nice people inside it." Two thugs dismounted and pulled the great barricade doors closed. Two others were lighting torches. Obviously, they weren't going to sit around and wait for me to accidently step through a detection gate again. Yusef carefully backed up and pulled me with him.

"Not good," he whispered. "If we shift now, they'll burn everything."

One of the drunks outside the saloon tipped up his hat. "I seen 'er. She went in the alley behind the tradin' post not more than ten minutes ago. I ain't seen her come out."

"Time to go." Yusef tried to pull me farther back.

"No, they've got to catch me. Otherwise they'll kill these people." I shoved the hobo-stick into his hand. "You can get out. Try to find one of my alternates in another reality. Make me be your friend. Goodbye." Before he could stop me, I ran out into the main street.

"I'm over here. Don't kill me." I pleaded, raising my hands as a sign of surrender.

The leader spun his horse around and pointed his rifle at my heart. The onlookers didn't try to help—they just stared.

"Ah, Miss Pawlak, the little refugee." He sneered. "I'm not going to kill you. Not here anyways. Arter wants to talk to you first."

Some of the other crooks dismounted and crowded in close.

Now that they had seen me, I could shift and these people would be safe. I still had the Big Brother plug in my pocket. I tried lowering my hand into my pocket, but he noticed. "Keep yer hands in the air, missy. No funny business." He shoved his rifle closer to me.

Another gunman shouted, "And you, ugly *Injun*, you better step back."

I looked behind me and my heart sank. Yusef had come out of hiding and was briskly marching up to us.

"I said get back Injun." The gunman took aim.

"No!" I yelled, but I was too far away to block the shot.

Just as the man cocked the hammer of his pistol, Yusef pulled my cell phone horseshoe out from my kerchief and threw it at him. It hit him smack in the forehead, and he fell off his horse like a rock. The next closest thug got the butt-end of the hobo-stick in his gut. His torch dropped into the muddy road and sputtered out. Time to fight our way out of here. The leader lifted his gun toward Yusef, but I pushed it up and it fired into the air. He growled in anger and grabbed my face, shoving me to the ground. He jumped off his horse and stood over me.

"Let me introduce myself. Name's Hill-Billy. Don't like it, you can complain to the boss-man when I take ya to 'im. Arter said don't kill ya. He didn't say nothin' about bringin' you back with all your toes." His heavy boot came down on my ankle and the rifle jabbed into the top of my shoe. I screamed.

Yusef had downed another crook, and he turned to the man above me and bashed him in the back with the stick. Hill-Billy let out a yelp and I dove out of the way. Another man, still on his horse, came galloping up to Yusef with his riffle poised, ready to club him on the head. Yusef stood right in the way. He stepped back just in time and swung the stick around. The kerchief full of plugs hit the man square on the neck. He and his horse disappeared. The crowd jumped and gasped in horror.

"Where'd ya send 'im?" Hill-Billy demanded, clutching his back as he stood up.

"A hundred different places at once. Tell Arter to leave us alone, or I'll send him there too." Yusef gripped the stick like a javelin and squared his jaw. The thugs on the ground groaned in pain and rolled over. They began arguing.

"Screw Arter. Let's just kill 'em."

"I'm not going get in trouble from Arter. No way."

"You are always such a wuss."

Yusef's eyes were animated. This was our chance to escape while they were distracted. He slowly crouched down to pick up the horseshoe that had fallen in the middle of the road. The men weren't watching. He dove over to me and wrapped his arms around me. I pulled the Big Brother plug out of my pocket.

"Hey, stop!" The gunmen quit quarrelling and came at us, aiming their guns.

I touched the plug to my neck just as I heard the blast of the gunshot.

Chapter 9

I blinked. Bright sun was filtering through the trees and onto a manicured lawn. I could hear laughter and I smelled club sandwiches and french-fries. I couldn't feel Yusef's arms. He was no longer there.

I looked around and saw the dorm and courtyard where students were lounging outside, eating lunch. This was the same spot where I'd shifted for the first time. So far, every shift I did was motivated by danger.

Thankfully, I had normal clothes on again. I was back.

Where was Yusef? He had the rest of the plugs. Had he transported to the place where he last shifted? He said he'd touched Arter's robes. But where had he been standing?

On instinct, I stood up and started walking over to the ped-way before I realized I should probably hide. I swerved into a clump of trees and peered out. I could see the courtyard, full of kids eating and talking. My stomach growled. Those subs looked good. I looked past the courtyard to the ped-way, but it was too far to see who was on it. Two teachers in black robes were sitting on a bench. It looked like all of the staff had adopted the Special Force uniform. They weren't eating, they were just watching. They were standing guard over the students, judging their every move. I was sure they were also there to keep watch for people like me.

How was I going to get past the sentinels? How would I find my friends? How would I escape? *Think.*

Then I saw Yusef. He was walking around the side of the fitness centre, wearing my backpack. I whistled to him from my hiding spot and he ducked into the trees.

"How did you get over here without setting off a detection gate?" I asked.

"I was outside when I shifted with Arter. I haven't gone through a gate."

I took a good look at him, back in his regular street clothes, but still sporting an awkward patch of stubble on his chin. I took my backpack and riffled through it to find every object amended. Swimsuit, towel, wallet, iPod. Back to normal.

"Where's my phone?" I asked.

"I don't know. It never appeared. Maybe it merged with itself."

"The last time I used it in this reality was to call my mom and try to tell her what was happening, but Arter picked it up. He probably still has it. Where's yours?"

"Back in the Wild West, in my cubbyhole under the stairs. It was a horseshoe. I don't usually carry those around in my pocket." He peaked over my head at the surveillance team on the bench.

"Crap. We need to find out where the others are."

Just then I saw Glynis's roommate Paula walking toward the dorms. "Paula," I called.

She stopped, not seeing me, wondering who had called her name.

"Over here." I beckoned from behind a tree.

She squinted at me. "Halina? I thought you were expelled. What are you doing here? Yusef? Where have you been for the last four days? They threatened to expel you too if you ever showed up again."

I bypassed all of her questions and asked my own. "Where is Glynis?"

"Expelled along with her popcorn boyfriend."

"And Jan? What about her?"

"Birds of a feather. Such a tight-knit little group you all are."

"Listen, Paula, I really need you to do me a favour. I need you to call Glynis's parents and ask them where she is. Can you do that for me?"

"Why don't you call?"

I smiled through clenched teeth. "Because I don't have a phone."

"Well, mine's in my dorm, so you'll have to come with me."

Yusef spoke up. "Can you go call and then come back and tell us?"

"Are you guys hiding or something? Am I going to regret helping you?"

"You'll never know if you don't try." I was starting to sound like that sticky sweet voice of RAS. "Please, Paula."

"I suppose...be right back," she said.

"Hey, are you gonna eat that?" Yusef pointed to a sub sandwich held under her arm.

"Help yourself." She tossed it to him as she sauntered off at a more than leisurely pace.

He broke it and gave half to me. "Oh, thank you." It literally took me fifteen seconds to eat it.

I turned to him. "By the way, nice rescue in the Wild West. What was that all about?"

"Uh, Torvald's been teaching me some stuff about confusing your opponents by exerting confidence even in the face of unlikely odds."

"I don't think he meant taking on six guys with guns."

"Well, it worked, didn't it?" He smiled.

I smiled back. "It was pretty awesome."

We waited forever for Paula to come back. Lunch break was almost over. When she finally returned, she looked a bit scared.

"Something really creepy is going on," she said.

"We know," Yusef and I said together.

"I talked with Glynis's parents, and they said she never made it home. Jan's parents said the same thing. I don't have Popcorn's phone number, but I bet it's the same. They said a bunch of parents of missing kids have launched an investigation—including yours and his." She tipped her head toward Yusef. "They said your parents received a phone call from you right before you were kidnapped. Apparently, the school is under suspicion, but nobody here has heard of that." She paused, looking me up and down. "You don't look kidnapped to me."

"It's complicated."

"Well, I'm sure your parents will be relieved that you're all right."

"You didn't tell them I was here, did you?" Panic rose in my stomach.

"Well, yeah, I figured they'd want to know."

"*Argh.* Paula."

"What?"

Just then, two cops and Principal Arter came out of the cafeteria and walked toward the teachers on the bench in the courtyard.

"Oh-oh. I think someone's notified the authorities," Yusef said.

"If the others aren't here, then they must have been exiled." I shook my head. Saving my friends from exile was not on my agenda and it wouldn't be on Yusef's agenda either.

"Do you have an Exile plug in here?" He grabbed my backpack and sifted through it.

I pulled it back and held it against my chest. No way. I would never let him go somewhere so dangerous. I stammered out a lie. "I don't know. I don't remember—"

"You guys are about to get caught," Paula interrupted.

The teachers on the bench stood up and began walking with the rest of the horde. They were on an interception course.

"If we shift together, we could end up separated again," I said, worried. "How do we find each other? We don't have our phones."

"With our luck they would end up as horseshoes again," Yusef said.

"Hey, that's a good idea. Let's go back to the Wild West. They won't be looking for us there. Those bad guys will be gone. And we know we'll be together. We'll be in the middle of the street."

"I don't know what you guys are talking about, but you better run before they see you," Paula said.

I found the Wild West plug, grabbed Yusef around the waist and gave her a sly smile. "You're the only one who can see us. We're ghosts."

"Boo." Yusef laughed as we shifted. Paula squealed.

Chapter 10

Dust sprayed into my mouth. Yusef yelled for me to move, and then he pushed me out of the way just as a horse and buggy ploughed through the main street of Fort Edmonton.

"Yikes." I scooted out of the road and looked at the two of us as pioneers. It was almost a relief to be back. At least we knew what was going on around here. No RAS. No Special Force.

"Let's go get my horseshoe." Yusef hoisted the hobo-stick over his shoulder and we breezed past the startled onlookers outside the saloon.

When we crept into the back of the trading post, the cashier was leaning over his counter yapping with his customers. "I knew that *Injun* was full of Blackfoot voodoo. He scooped up that poor redheaded missy and whisked her away to no-man's-land. Who knows what kinda curse he left on all my goods in the back. He touched every single one of 'em." The customers guffawed at his story telling, but they all clammed up when they saw Yusef coming up from behind.

"I curse you, Mr. Aims, to go deaf." Yusef grabbed him and boxed his ears.

Aims jumped so high that he hit his head on the chandelier.

"Blackfoot voodoo magic," one of the patrons screamed. They all started stampeding for the door.

Mr. Aims was crying like a girl. "I can't hear. I can't hear nothing."

"Serves you right for treating me like a dog." We were laughing so hard we couldn't stand up straight.

"Come on, you Indian, we better find your magic horseshoe," I teased.

"Lina, we have to think about how we are going to do this. We can't shift together. You saw what happened last time. We could end up anywhere our alternate selves are."

"Well, I don't want you to get stuck somewhere that I can't find you."

"We're gonna have to split up. Give me half of the plugs. We'll have to hope that by the time we've jumped to every reality, we'll find each other again."

I did not like this idea. It was so improbable—like putting a coin in the jellybean machine and hoping you get all the black ones.

"That will never work," I told him. "We would have to have two plugs that are the same to end up in the same place, and it would have to be somewhere neither of us had alternate selves."

"It's a process of elimination. The more realities we go to, the fewer alternates we have. By merging with each one, the possibilities of our location decreases. We'll meet each other right here, downtown Edmonton. I'm guessing we're close to the museum."

"If the museum exists. This isn't like sneaking in the dorm windows. Yusef, we can't do this."

"Yes, Lina, we can." He took me by the shoulders and looked straight into my eyes. "Dorm windows were just a warm up to this."

He was right.

"If Gerome—Coach Tyler—gave me a plug to Safe Place, then he must have had one too. That means there is more than one plug to each reality. We just have to find them."

I dumped out all of the plugs. None were a matching pair. We would never meet up. This was a crazy and stupid plan.

A loud thump banged against the outside wall. People outside were arguing and yelling something about voodoo. Something thumped against the building again.

"We better go," I said.

"Give me the number to Safe Place. I'll have to find a plug with the same number and I'll meet you there.

"How?"

"I don't know. I'll figure that out."

"You are leaving way too much up to chance." Small beads of sweat were dripping down my forehead.

"We don't have a choice." Yusef was sweating too.

I took a deep breath. Coach Tyler always said breathing was the most important thing to do in an emergency. Separating the plugs into two piles, I gave half to him and kept the other half. I sorted through them until I saw the Exile plug. It gave me a terrible feeling. Yusef was *not* going there alone. I carefully closed it in my fist so Yusef wouldn't get it. We wrapped his plugs in a potato sack with his horseshoe.

He said the Safe Place number to himself a few times so he wouldn't forget it. He took a deep, slow breath and said, "Okay."

I backed up to make sure I wasn't touching him. He pulled out a random plug. The look in his eyes was the same look he gave me when he was trying to pull me out the dorm window—helpless. Then he was gone. I had a feeling of foreboding, like I could be waiting at the museum forever and he would never show up.

Chapter 11

I opened my eyes. The first thing I noticed was the grey and white polyester jumpsuit I was wearing. It had ribbed stitching wrapped around every joint—like something out of Star Trek. Like some army issue yoga instructor's outfit. Like Lulu Lemon and an alien got it on and had a really ugly baby. It didn't appear to have zippers, buttons, or any other way to get out of it. My usually bouncy red hair was pinned tightly to my head, and I was wearing frameless glasses with no prescription.

I looked around and saw that the walls, floor and ceiling were made of some type of thick, luminescent glass. I barely saw through it to the hallway beyond. I slid open the glass door. The hallway was full of windows with rounded corners. I could easily see through them to the blackness beyond—the blackness of outer space.

I *was* in Star Trek. I was on some futuristic space station. All the people walking through the hall had on the same clothes, same hairstyle and same glasses.

"Where am I?" I murmured. As soon as I spoke, my glasses lit up with a glowing, three dimensional map of the space station. A red dot showed my location in one of the outer corridors. I almost fell backward. I pulled the glasses off. They looked normal except for a moving map lit up on the lenses. I put them back on.

People were giving me sideways glances, so I started walking down the corridor. I must have looked conspicuous, because a moment later, a tall dark haired woman stopped me.

"Excuse me, I don't recognize you. What clone are you?"

"Huh?"

"What is your name, dear?" she said in a friendly voice.

"Umm, Lina."

She tilted her head to the side. "Are you new? I didn't think we had a Lina." She stared into her glasses and I noticed columns of data scrolling over the lenses, but it was too small for me to read. When the scrolling stopped, she peered down at me. I saw an imprint glisten on her neck. "Where did you come from?"

"You mean what reality?" I said slowly, "047829."

"047829," she repeated and lights flickered in her glasses. "Do you have a plug?"

I reached for my backpack, but the shoulder straps were missing. I felt along my back and realized my pack was attached to my clothes. The woman grabbed the pack from the bottom and pulled a ripcord. The pack came loose.

"Thanks." The pack held on with magnetic clasps. I peeked up and noticed for the first time that everyone had a magnetic pack on their backs. I rummaged around until I remembered that I'd given it to Yusef.

"Umm, I don't have it."

"How were you planning to get back?"

"I wasn't planning on going back."

She paused, studying me. "Well, I'm going to have to take you to the main deck. Follow me."

The map to the main deck shone in my glasses. I shrugged my shoulders. This woman appeared helpful, so what was there to lose? At least she wasn't pointing some Trekkie taser at my face.

People stared directly at me as we walked, and after we passed them, they whispered to each other.

"It's always exciting to have new DNA, since stealing it would be unlawful—we have to wait for it to be volunteered." She squinted. "You will volunteer, won't you?"

"Volunteer for what?"

"Your DNA. It's just a blood sample."

"What do you need my DNA for?"

She started walking again, this time a bit faster. "Captain Thomas will explain everything."

I wanted to ask more questions, but I kept my mouth shut.

The corridor continued to gently curve around the edge of the space station—the place was massive. Occasionally the wall would give way to a great, open area full of people. They were staring into their glasses as they listened to a man speaking at a pulpit. They were a flood of white and grey.

"Are you hungry? Maybe we should stop by the mess hall first."

"I'm starving," I answered.

"By the way, my name is Carmen." She picked up my hand and shook it.

Carmen took me into a glass elevator in a glass tube. It reminded me of the glass tubes full of plugs—it even evaporated in the same way when I touched it—it made me suspicious. Why did they have the same technology as Special Force?

The mess hall was huge. A buffet stood in the middle, covered with platters of fresh fruits and vegetables, baking, salads, even pizza. White tables surrounded the buffet, seating hundreds of hungry people.

"You might be wondering how we acquired all of this produce. We don't grow it here on the Station. We have a reality we like to call the Garden of Eden. It is mostly tended to by the Shelleys. She is our best gardener. We have a few colonies there, but the place is a secret. The Special Force doesn't know about it, and we need to keep it that way." Carmen piled food onto her plate and beckoned me to do likewise.

"You can hide realities from them?" I asked, following her down the line.

"Sure, as long as they don't have the number. Eventually they may find it. They have the same RAS system as we do, so if they found out the Real Status number for Garden of Eden they could make their own plug. Then we would end up at war with them, just like we are here." She sat down at an empty table.

"So, have you got a big computer that looks like flowing blue lava?" I popped food into my mouth.

She tapped her glasses. "Our glasses are networked to every RAS in every reality. The blue lava thing is an old technology. The audio response got sickening after a while."

A woman walking to a nearby table called out to her. "Hey, Carmen, who are you with?"

Carmen responded, "I'll tell you after she's had her orientation."

"Okay. How exciting." The woman led her group of friends away from us.

I looked closely at the woman—same brown hair and brown eyes as Carmen, only she was a few years younger.

"Is she your sister?" I asked.

Carmen smiled. "Everything will make sense after your orientation. Now eat your lunch."

I obeyed, feeling uneasy.

Chapter 12

Captain Thomas stood in front of a large convex window, hands clasped behind his back. His grey and white uniform accentuated his broad shoulders and large frame. A balcony loomed over the opposite wall, where people sat in high chairs, talking to their glasses and typing on keyboards. Bubbles of glass protruded from the walls with detailed graphs and charts lit up on them.

"Carmen, what have you brought me?" He turned as we approached.

"L-I-N-A from 048297."

The Captain's glasses lit up. "Says here that Reality is run by the Special Force. Tell me, Lina, how did you break free?"

I put my hands on my hips. "Before I tell you anything, I want some of my questions answered."

The Captain chuckled. "Spunky, isn't she? She might be well placed in espionage or avionics."

Carmen smiled. "I was thinking ballistics."

"You're not putting me anywhere. I have to help—"

"Of course not, dear." Thomas smiled.

"How did I end up on board a space station? I was in Alberta, Canada when I shifted."

"You need to let me explain." Thomas led us to a cluster of chairs near the back of the room.

We sat down.

"You are in the same position in the galaxy as you were in Canada. We have the space station hovering in earth's orbit in case we had shifters coming from other realities. We wouldn't want you floating out in space, now would we?"

My heart squeezed inside my chest. "What happened to the planet?"

"It was destroyed by the Special Force. They had too much opposition from those of us unwilling to conform. We had very few survivors. It was necessary to begin cloning in order to keep our numbers up. The Special Force has a large fleet of vessels. They can clone faster than we can—they have more DNA to work with. Plus they have broken the *Freedom of Information and Privacy Protection Act.* They will shift to other realities to acquire DNA by force. This is highly unethical from our standpoint. That is why we are so glad to see you, dear. We need you to volunteer. Every bit of new blood helps."

"May we scan your imprint?" Carmen asked. She unhooked her pack and pulled out a tiny scanner.

"Why?"

"To see your shifting history, as well as monitor where you go and how many alternate selves you merge with."

They were patiently putting up with my scepticism, so I relaxed my guard. I nodded. She scanned me and her glasses lit up.

"Only one merge so far." Carmen let out a sigh of relief.

"You are lucky," Thomas said to me. "Merging too many times can cause serious side effects."

"Like what?" I thought about Yusef and where he might be at this moment.

"Merging begins to create alternate memories. If you pile on too many lifetimes of memories, you can start to forget who you really are. It can drive a person insane. It is dangerous to exceed more than ten."

Carmen tilted her head. "Not only that, but the family and friends that you leave behind in each reality will suffer your loss. They will think you are dead."

I thought about the search party my parents had sent out. And now my alternate parents in Safe Place would think I am missing. Shifting no longer held a sense of intrigue and adventure. I had to end this. "Can you help me locate some of my friends?"

Carmen shrugged. "Possibly. If we could scan them. Give us their names and maybe we have their DNA."

"Jan Kurauchi."

A list of names scrolled quickly in my glasses. Captain Thomas and Carmen were receiving the same information. Pictures appeared of several girls who had the same name, but none of them was her.

"No, that's not right." My glasses followed my command, bringing up the next image.

"There. That's Jan." A chart appeared. It had a list of Statuses and corresponding realities.

Reality 047829—Status: Stationary.

Reality 047941—Status: Stationary.

It kept going. "What about here? Is she here?"

Reality 53091—Status: Deceased.

"Deceased. What does that mean?"

"It means she was probably on the planet when it was destroyed." Carmen's eyes were full of sympathy.

I pinched the bridge of my nose. "Okay, what about Yusef Hassam?"

Reality 53091—Status: Deceased.

I punched the chair.

Carmen put her hand on my shoulder. "It is hard to see such a status, but remember they are still alive in other realities."

"I know." I tried Glynis and Torvald with the same results.

"What about Spencer Wright?"

"Yes, we have a Spencer. Is this the correct one?" Carmen's lenses transferred data instantly to mine.

His face popped up. "It's him."

"Locate the nearest Spencer and invite him to the main deck," Thomas spoke aloud.

I could see a map with a small red dot in his glasses.

"These glasses are really cool." I pulled them off my face to analyze them.

Our version of the Real Administration System is the most advanced in any reality," Carmen said.

That was for sure.

She continued, "RAS was initially built here. We intended it to stay here, but the designs were leaked to the Special Force, which began sneaking copies into other realities. We try to stop them whenever we can, but many realities are already overrun. If you have the glasses, you don't even need plugs to shift. Of course, they will turn into regular specs in realities where RAS doesn't exist."

"Yeah, my cell phone turned into a horseshoe."

"What's a cell phone?" Carmen asked.

Spencer walked into the room before I could answer her. I ran over to him and gave him a hug. "Spence. It is good to see you, man. This is a crazy place."

He frowned at me. "I don't recognize you. You must have me confused with another Spencer. I am Spencer number 4606." He indicated the number that was stitched into the shoulder of his uniform.

Curious, I glanced at my own suit. It said number one.

"You're a clone? Really? No way, you look just like him." He had the same voice, same smile, even the same spiky haircut.

"That's the idea. There are seventeen other Spencers on board the Earth Station—one hundred and twenty-two on other vessels. The original DNA was lost during planet destruction."

"Oh. Well, it's good to see someone who looks like one of my friends."

"Thank you, Spencer." The captain placed a hand on his shoulder. "You may return to your station."

"Thank you, sir." He formally addressed the captain, but his shield went down for a moment when he turned and whispered to me, "Sorry about whatever happened to your friend. If it's any consolation, I could find it very easy to be friends with you." He threw me a guns sign with his fingers before he walked away.

I turned to Thomas. "Why did you show him to me?"

"To help you trust us. The clones don't have original memories, but they do maintain personality. If you know that the original Spencer would be behind our cause, then you know his clones would make the same choices."

"Lina." Carmen stepped forward. We would be very appreciative if you could donate your DNA."

"Yeah, okay. But I would like to ask a favour of you. I want to find my original friends, the ones I know from 047829. Can I—"

"You can find them easily by finding one of their alternates and making them shift back to 047829. They will merge and eventually their memories will come back to them. It is not particularly ethical, and sometimes the alternates can be...reluctant."

"But what if their alternate doesn't have an imprint?" I thought of Jan back at Safe Place.

"You don't need an imprint to shift. You just need to be touching someone who has one. Whatever is touching you comes with you. Otherwise, you would be naked when you showed up here."

"Ugh." I said, trying to drive the image of a naked Arter out of my head.

Captain Thomas touched my shoulder. "Lina, you should know that our spies in 047829 have discovered the Special Force has already infiltrated most national governments. You should permanently shift out of there."

"That's why I need to find my friends. And what about my parents?"

"Bring them with you if you can, but you can't save everyone in every reality."

Where had I heard that before?

"Carmen-96, please bring me some Earth Station plugs, say, about four?"

Thomas wasn't looking at Carmen when he spoke and she didn't move from her chair. I thought she hadn't heard him until another woman came down the steps from the balcony. It was another Carmen. The second Carmen handed the plugs to Thomas, smiled and went back to her station. Both women said nothing to each other; they hardly even looked at each other. They acted as if it was completely normal to work alongside their identical twin.

Thomas touched my shoulder again. "Take these. When you find your friends, please, bring them back here. Even if you don't stay, at least we can persuade them to give their DNA."

I took the plugs. "Can they come here if they were already killed here? Wouldn't they end up buried in a grave somewhere?"

"A shifter would never merge with a deceased body. Besides, the people on earth were completely obliterated." He smiled. "You made it here, didn't you?"

I gulped. "What is the status of Halina Pawlak, Home Reality Earth Station?"

My picture was the first to appear on my lenses.

Reality 53091—Status: Deceased.

I blinked. *I'm dead?*

Chapter 13

"Come with me, Lina. I will take you to the extraction unit."
Carmen tugged on my elbow, asking me to stand. The status on my
glasses faded away, replaced by another map with a red dot above the
extraction unit. As I walked, I wondered how many realities would show
my status as deceased. It was morbid to think about the earth blowing up
with all my friends and family on it. How many other ways and times
had I died? I knew the glasses could tell me, but I didn't want to check.

"Lina," Carmen called.

We were walking into the centre of the Earth Station. The hallways
were getting brighter, like light was coming right out of the glass walls.
To the left, the glass became clear, showing the next room beyond.
People dressed in white lab coats observed tall glass tubes full of
yellowish liquid. Carmen saw me staring.

"This is the cloning unit." She pointed to the tubes. "The liquid is
unassigned human tissue. When we assign DNA to the tissue, it takes
only a few days to form the shape of a complete human body."

"It looks like phlegm," I said.

"It's more like plasma."

"Do you start the clones as babies?" I asked.

"We could. It just isn't necessary here on this station. We are set up
for offensive operations, not as a nursery. There are other stations that
are more accommodating to children."

"How do you control it? The aging?"

"It all depends on how much tissue we use. There are different sized
forms made of a carbon-based material. The liquid tissue is slowly
poured over the form. If we use seven pounds of tissue and pour it over a

newborn form, there would be a baby, but we don't carry those forms here. We would pour one hundred and twenty pounds of tissue over an adult form to make a clone of you. It is best to build a clone in its prime."

"Where do you get the phlegm from?"

"That isn't a pleasant topic. Let's just say, we have had many casualties in this war."

"So, basically you are recycling people?" The thought was gross, but also logical.

"In the best sense." She tugged my arm to suggest we continue.

"Can the clones get pregnant?" I was much too curious to end the conversation.

"Yes, and their offspring becomes a new strain of DNA that can also be cloned. It is a valuable addition to our numbers, but not encouraged on the war stations. Pregnant women have to transfer off the station for their protection. Personally, I would never risk losing my position. The war would have to end before I considered raising a family."

"So, do they get transferred to another reality to have their babies?"

"Most of the time. Our stations that cater to families are kept well hidden from the Special Force. I've never been there. Some of my clones have had babies, so I know what my children might have looked like."

"You're not a clone?"

She stopped and tilted her head. "No. I am Carmen de Portue from 77295. I shifted here eight years ago and I never left." She proudly displayed her number one crest.

"You've never gone back?" I asked.

"It's not worth it. Here we still have a fighting chance. I wouldn't recommend going to my home unless you really want to see a world where the Special Force has control of everything."

As we walked in silence, a phrase kept going through my mind like a looped recording. *I can't save everyone in every reality. I can't save everyone in every reality.* I had to focus on the people I could save. I had to focus on my friends and my family.

I looked up at Carmen as she walked in front of me. Her black hair was in a tight bun, but I could imagine that hair flowing down over her shoulders. She had saved herself from the terrible fascist society of the Special Force, the same society that my home reality would turn into if I didn't do something soon.

More questions began surging through my head. Where were the people I knew who were behind all of this? I had to monitor my enemies.

"Show me the location of Jacque Arter," I asked my RAS glasses. Even before his picture popped up, Carmen whirled around and glared at me. Her eyes were on fire.

"What did you say?"

His location read, Main deck of Special Force vessel, *The Charger*.

"I'm just curious about the location—"

She cut me off. "You never did tell us how you escaped a reality already occupied by Special Force. Perhaps you didn't escape at all. Perhaps they *let* you go." Her glasses were lighting up with unreadable words.

I shouldn't have said Arter's name in front of her. Of course he would be as dangerous here as in any other reality. "Do you get spies trying to shift here?"

Her fiery eyes bore into me even deeper. "Not often. How do you know Arter?"

"He's the principal at my school. He's with Special Force."

"Of course he is. All of his alternates think the same." She let out a huff. "Is there anyone else there that we should know about?"

"G-Gerome...um...Tyler. He's my swim coach." His photo popped up in front of my eyes. My heart sank at the sight of him.

Gerome Tyler, Home Reality 047829—Status: Transition.

"That's not possible." Carmen was viewing the same screen.

"What does transition mean?"

"It means he has been here and left. Only a detection gate or an imprint scan can clock a person's whereabouts. We haven't scanned him, and only the Special Force has detection gates. If he shifted here, he didn't come to us. Is there a chance someone followed you here?"

"Coach Tyler? Why would he? He was just my swim coach." As soon as I said it, I knew I was lying—mostly to myself.

"Were you being chased?" Carmen stepped closer to me, the lights scrolling in her glasses reflected off her pupils.

"I thought they couldn't follow me." My voice was shaking.

She scowled at me as if I was a naive child. "If Tyler snuck in here and hid a detection gate somewhere, then he could find you. He could find anyone with an imprint. The Special Force has attempted this before."

She touched her glasses. "Possible security breach. Scan entire vessel for location gates." As soon as she spoke, the entire station rang with alarms. The white lights plunged into red. People dropped whatever they were doing and pulled out scanners from their packs. As they swept the area for gates, they called out locations on the map in their glasses.

"Left wing clone unit entrance, negative. Right wing clone unit entrance, negative." Everyone was talking at once. Every check logged itself instantly into RAS. It looked like a well-rehearsed drill.

"Don't move." Carmen pulled her own scanner out and swept it over and around me. She began listing the names of hallways and elevators, retracing our path all the way back to the hallway she found me in.

After a tense moment, the red lights brightened to white. My glasses read, *All Clear*. Carmen closed her eyes and sighed.

"How often does that happen?" I asked.

"Often enough. Come on, we need to get you to extraction." She moved down the hallway.

I followed. "You're just taking blood right?" The term "extraction" was beginning to sound scary.

She gave me a tilted smile, but she said nothing. She walked silently until we reached the extraction unit door. "This is where I leave you. I have other duties to attend to. Thank you again for your support, Lina." And with that, she left.

I pushed open the door. The lab techs were expecting me. They took a sample of my blood. They measured and weighed me. Nobody talked beyond casual conversation, if you assume asking about the weather on your home reality was casual conversation. It felt like I was in a doctor's office. I guess I was.

Soon I was released back out into the hallway. I retraced my steps to the cloning unit and watched for a while. The lab tech who had taken my blood came into the room carrying a large glass tube. She put it into an incubator. They sure didn't waste any time.

Without warning, my body was jolted forward and I smacked my face against the glass. A loud explosion shook the hallway accompanied by a deafening crack. I pushed myself off the window and plugged my ears. The lighting switched to red once again.

"Carmen, what's happening?" I said aloud, hoping my glasses could call to her. They lit up with the word *Warning* flashing in red. A siren bellowed, but it was repeatedly drowned out by cracking explosions.

Earth Station is within range of Special Force offensive vessel, The Charger. Taking evasive action.

Others were jogging around, talking to their glasses and scrolling through screens. I peered into the red lights of the lab. The technicians were securing the incubators. They looked well practiced, as though they had dealt with this many times before. It gave me some reassurance, until I saw the lab tech with my DNA touch the incubator and disappear with it. She was shifting to protect the DNA. Two more technicians did the same thing. This must be part of the drill, I thought, standard procedure.

The hallway shook again and tilted downward. The floor became a ramp. I trotted down it until I came to an exterior window. There, right in front of me, was a massive ship. A battle ship. It reminded me of an American destroyer without a rudder. Thick steal wings came jutting out the sides, and massive rocket boosters crossed the top and bottom. It was the size of a football field.

Carmen's picture appeared in my glasses. "Lina, this is not a good time for you to be here. You should shift back home if it is safe."

"It's not safe," I replied.

"Do you have a reality where it is safe? Remember, try not to merge again if you can help it. If there is an RAS computer, you can keep your glasses."

I tried to think where I could go. Safe Place popped into my mind. "Yeah, I know where to go. I'll come back here if I can."

"Thanks, Lina." Her picture disappeared.

I went to grab my pack, but remembered I didn't need a plug. I spoke to my glasses. "Show me my shift history." The numbers popped up. "Send me to Safe Place number 346181." Then I disappeared too.

Chapter 14

I opened my eyes and found myself in Gerome's office. I crouched down to hide myself in case anyone was around. My clothes and backpack were back to normal. What day was it? Was he working today? I had no idea. It felt like it had been weeks since I'd been here.

I still had my glasses. I tested them. The message on the lenses was archaic looking compared to the high quality on the space station. I immediately realized why. I was seeing the same screen as Gerome's secret computer.

"What day is it?" I whispered.

Tuesday.

"Show me the location of Gerome Tyler."

Gerome Tyler, Location: 047829

I relaxed my shoulders. Peeking over the edge of his desk, I could see the pool in the room beyond. Empty. No swim club on Tuesday. I looked at the clock. 5:00 pm. Everyone would be in the cafeteria, but public swim was in an hour. I formed a plan in my mind. I would find Jan. Shift with her back home and then shift back out. That way she would merge with her alternate self and eventually regain her memory.

I picked up the phone on Gerome's desk and dialled her cell number. Behind me, I heard a quiet ringing. It was coming from the secret room behind the lockers. I pushed the door open and peered inside. Sitting on the desk, a phone was lit up. It was Jan's. Had she left it there on purpose? My mind filled with dread. Had she been caught?

I hung up both phones. Grabbing hers in my hand, I noticed a text message she had sent to herself. I knew her password, so I opened it.

Identity still safe. Send word.

"How can I phone you if I have your phone?" I whispered to myself.

I closed the locker and approached the office door, but stopped when I caught a glint of a band of silver over the doorway. The detection gate. I forgot about it. I couldn't get out of the office. My hand went to the bridge of my nose. *I've got to stop doing that.* I put my hand down. I had to break the window to get out. Then I would really be in a hurry. I had to know where Jan was before I smashed the glass.

I dialled the number of the only other person I knew. I just hoped he would actually talk to me this time.

"Hello?"

I could hear echoing noises, people talking, chairs sliding. He must be in the cafeteria.

"Hey, Yusef, it's Halina."

"Halina? Why are you calling me?"

"I'm looking for Jan, have you seen her?"

"No."

"Are you at supper? Is she there?"

"I don't see her."

"I need you to look for her, it's really important."

"Why did you call me? Why don't you call Spencer?"

"Um, I don't know his number. Please Yusef, I need your help."

He paused.

"Just a sec."

A minute later, he came back on the line. "Yeah, she's still in the line."

I could have jumped for joy. "Thanks so much, I owe you one." I was about to hang up.

"Halina? What's this all about?"

"It's such a long story...it won't make any sense to you."

"Try me."

I stopped. I didn't have time for this. Was I obligated to tell him? I thought about our meeting in the computer lab. He said we hadn't talked since middle school. I tried to remember why. A flood of images filled my mind, images of an awkward, skinny girl in a bathing suit.

I was at the county pool in Victoria with my parents. I was showing them the stroke I was learning—the butterfly. Then, a young, scrawny version of Yusef came through the change room doors. His dark skin dotted with goose bumps. Being seen in a bathing suit was a terrifying thought to me. I dunked my head under the water to hide, but when I came back to the surface, he was standing right in front of me. I squealed and covered my flat chest with my arms.

"Halina, can you teach me how to swim?"

"What? No. That's what lessons are for, dummy."

My mom smiled. "Lina, why not? You could just show him some basic—"

"No. I'm too tired. I'm too cold. I want to be done." I'm too embarrassed was more like it. I didn't get out of the pool until I was sure Yusef had turned away.

"What's wrong, Lina? You aren't usually so shy." My mother handed me a towel.

The twelve-year-old me didn't have an answer for her, but maybe the seventeen year old me did.

"Lina? Are you there?"

He called me Lina. I don't know why, but it was so nice to hear it.

"Yeah. Yusef, I'm so sorry we haven't kept...I mean, I'm sorry I didn't work harder at our friendship. It was hard, you know?"

"Sure, whatever."

"No, not whatever. I missed out on some good times. I was just embarrassed about...some stuff."

"*You* were embarrassed?"

I paused. This was so uncomfortable. Why was I having this conversation? I was on a strict schedule. I didn't have time for this, but Yusef was opening up to me. If I sloughed him off now, he might shut down. What was I thinking? This was a different Yusef. An alternate Yusef. I already had his friendship. In fact, he had saved my life. So why did it feel so important to bond with his alternate?

"Yeah, well, puberty isn't the greatest time to have guy friends." I felt my cheeks flare with heat.

"Especially at the swimming pool, right?"

Oh my goodness. He was thinking of the same thing—the alternate memory I had so recently acquired.

"How do you think I felt, knowing I couldn't swim and I was asking a girl to teach me? Do you know how long I sat in the dressing room, building up the courage to ask you?"

"Listen, I'm sorry. It wasn't a good time for both of us. Can I make it up to you?"

"I already learned how to swim. I went and took lessons, dummy."

Ouch. I looked out at the empty pool and cringed. Yusef was stubborn. It would take a lot of effort to gain his friendship again.

"Can we talk about this another time?" I looked at the clock. It was 5:30.

"You know my number."

Click.

I felt sick. I tried to tell myself this wasn't real, this wasn't the real

Yusef, but how could I say that? Of course he was real. If I was about to merge Jan's alternate, then why wouldn't I want to merge Yusef? I concluded he would never want to—I didn't feel like it was my responsibility.

Enough of this. Stop thinking so much. I looked at the window that was trapping me in Gerome's office and it made me furious. I couldn't handle all this pressure. I felt like I was going to burst.

"I can't save everyone," I yelled, hoisting the chair over my head and pounded it against the glass. The crash exploded through the whole room. Glass shattered everywhere. I ducked my head as I heard shards scatter all over the desk and the tiles on the pool room floor.

I crawled onto the desk and dropped down onto the tiles, taking a quick glance back at the detection gate to make sure I hadn't set it off. I picked my way through the glass and headed to the ped-way where I could hear members of the swim team coming down the hallway.

My heart thumped. Once the broken window was discovered, I would have a very narrow margin of time. Tightening the straps on my backpack, I ran to the cafeteria.

Chapter 15

Jan was just returning her tray when I found her. Half a bun lay on top and I snatched up before she even saw me.

"Lina." She dropped the tray, bouncing utensils on the floor. She hugged me, stepping on her tray to get to me. "How did you get back? When did you get glasses?"

I shoved the bun in my mouth and gave her an incoherent answer.

"What?"

"I need to snag some food." I picked her tray up off the floor and butted in line to grab some sustenance. The last time I ate, I was on a space station.

She followed me. "Did you find my phone? After you left me in that secret room, I figured you might go back there. When I peeked out, everyone was gone. I snuck out and acted as if nothing happened. What's been going on the last couple of days? I wasn't sure if you'd ever make it back. I've been going nuts, but nobody else noticed you were missing since it was the weekend."

"Not even my parents?" I asked, picking up three bananas and shoving them in my backpack.

"They didn't call or anything." She grabbed a packaged sub and a bottle of water for me.

The intercom beeped. "Would Halina Pawlak please come see me in my office immediately," a female voice announced. The principal?

"Maybe they did notice," Jan said.

"No, that's for breaking the window. We've got to leave."

"What window?"

Jan followed me as I jogged out of the cafeteria. When I reached the door, I halted abruptly. Jan bumped into my back.

Yusef sat at the last table with a photo-shop manual in his hand, but he wasn't reading it. He watched me, his black eyes studying me as if I was a virus.

What could I say? "How are you?" That was lame.

"Are you in some sort of trouble?"

Jan huffed. "You could say that."

He looked at her.

"You won't believe it, Yusef. I didn't believe it."

I cleared my throat. "I broke the window to Ger—Coach Tyler's office."

Jan turned to me. "You did?"

"The office window at the pool?" Yusef said, overlapping Jan. "Was this before our conversation or after?" He set down his book and waited for my answer.

"Um, after."

The impact of my words was too great for him. He picked up his book and buried his face in it. The intercom came on again.

"If any student knows the whereabouts of Halina Pawlak, please alert security immediately."

A multitude of students turned their blank faces toward me.

"You better go," I heard Yusef mutter from behind his book.

"We'll talk later, okay?" I didn't hear him answer. I lost sight of him as Jan pushed me out the door.

"We need to go somewhere safe," Jan said as we ran down the hall. "Somewhere off campus." Students stared at us as we passed.

"Hey, Lina," someone called, "what did you do?"

Jan steered me to the first door outside. We could see the corner of the dormitory, but security guards were already going inside. We changed direction. I put my hood over my head to hide my telltale hair.

"Where can we go?" Jan asked. I didn't know the city that well. I felt lost. It made me want to go home.

After three blocks, we arrived at Whyte Avenue. It was pretty much the only place in the city that I *did* know. We hung out in the coffee shops afterschool, shopped in the eclectic curios, snuck out to the clubs. I saw the cafe where Gerome and I used to meet, and pursed my lips as we ran past it. Jan reminded me about a seedy motel six blocks down and we both agreed to go there.

As we quickened our pace, I explained my plan.

"Apparently, you don't need an imprint as long as I travel with you. We won't end up together. You've been caught. Maybe they have some sort of holding cell. I'll show up by the courtyard." I gave her the plug to

Safe Place. "Shift back here as soon as you can. You might be with some other people named Glynis and Torvald. They might give you some problems, but try to convince them to come with you. You just have to be touching them to shift back."

"If we had known that before, it might have saved us some problems." Jan was huffing with exertion.

I stopped.

"I don't need to rest, keep going," she said.

"It's not that. I need to warn you. If you merge, you'll disappear from the other reality. Your parents, your family, they won't know what happened. They'll think you're dead."

She looked up at me, "But those aren't my real parents. I'll be back here in no time. Come on."

"They *are* your real parents. Once you merge, you'll start getting alternate memories of them."

We watched as a police car parted the traffic and sped toward the campus, siren on, lights flashing. A second later, another cop car came through.

"Let's worry about that later. We gotta move." Jan tugged me forward.

As we arrived at the motel, Jan's phone rang. It was still in my pocket.

"Hello?"

"I hope you're not still on campus."

"Yusef?" I couldn't believe he was calling.

"You're in a lot of crap, Lina. The pool's closed down. It's considered a crime scene. There are cops questioning everybody. So far no one has spilled the beans."

I looked over to Jan. She was checking us in using her parents' emergency credit card.

"I'm a ways away, but I don't think it will take them long to find me. Can you make up a story for me?"

"What?"

"Can you cover for me? Say I was kidnapped or something."

During the long pause that followed, I could hear a pen tapping on a desk. He did that when he was thinking.

"You need to get rid of your phone."

"It's Jan's."

"Then don't answer it again. You were hit over the head in Coach Tyler's office and you don't remember anything."

Click.

I was worried, yet my mouth curled into a smile. Good ol' Yusef, up to his old tricks.

Jan got the keys and we went upstairs. The motel was a dive. The wallpaper was yellow, the ceiling had water stains and the floor creaked.

Jan scrunched her nose. "I don't even want to guess what kind of people stay here."

"Probably desperate people trying to escape the law."

She scowled at me.

We opened the door to our room and cringed. Two single beds, a nightstand and a TV were the only furnishings. The carpet must have been fifty years old and I was unsure of its original color. The bedspreads were a horrible blue, with a peach pattern that resembled slashes of paint. An airbrushed picture of an albino tiger hung on the wall.

"This is tacky," I said.

"Where else can we go where no one will see us?" Jan replied. She placed the *Do not disturb* sign on the outer handle, then closed and locked the door.

"Let's get out of here fast." I grabbed her hand. "Remember, you'll be imprisoned somewhere..."

"I remember. Just do it."

I couldn't help but smile at her eagerness.

I shifted into the familiar clump of trees. The pine needles looked sprayed with sparkles. The sun made the frost shimmer like tiny crystals. The world looked exactly the same. I wasn't fooled though. I knew this world held a destructive society inbred into the system whose purpose was to weed out the people who didn't meet their elitist standards. I also knew they wanted me dead for defying their human breeding project. Campus was probably a bad place for me to lounge around.

I could go anywhere in this reality and always end up back at the motel. Traveling was inconsequential. I decided I would go to the museum and see if, by chance, Yusef had left a message for me. I walked north to the Light Rail Transit Station. I didn't have a pass or change for the fare, but if I were lucky, they wouldn't check. If I could make it to the bridge without getting caught, I would make it across the river before they could boot me off. I slid into a plastic, bowl-shaped seat and slouched down. So far so good.

I stared out the window as the LRT glided across the river. The water ran swiftly down the middle of the North Saskatchewan River, even though the edges were crusted with dirty ice. I thought about the time a few days ago when I had to cross the river on a ferry in a Laura Ingalls dress. Things were so different between realities. Shifting gave me a major culture shock. I always thought I was good at adapting to new situations, but I wasn't prepared for something like this.

The science of shifting went so far beyond quantum mechanics I had no idea what to call it. I was in reaction mode, following my instincts without taking time to think about what I was doing. I didn't *know* anything—not at all. I just knew how I felt. My brain couldn't explain it. Things were rushing by so fast I couldn't keep up. They were rushing like the middle of the river and I was swimming against the current.

I looked up as an LRT officer opened the door at the far end of the car. I cursed. I would have to get off even though I was still two stops away from the museum. I watched him from under my hoodie as he approached the nearest person. He wasn't checking for tickets. He was scanning neck imprints. The transit system was already under the control of the Special Force. What else did those idiots have their hands in?

I had to get off before he scanned me and found out who I was. I stood up and walked to the front door. He eyed me suspiciously. The next station came into view and I sighed. I stepped off, shoving my hands into my pockets to avoid the chill. The tall skyscrapers were a blaze of gold in the setting sun. Again, my mind compared the modern downtown core to the plank boardwalk of the Wild West town square. Even with all of their differences, both places stilled smelled like crap.

The double doors of the Alberta Museum were floor to ceiling glass, with a herd of Bison etched across them. I remembered coming here once with Glynis so she could do some research for a history project. I chuckled to myself, thinking about how much research she could do in the Wild West. That was what I called hands-on experience.

"I'm sorry, but the museum is closing in ten minutes," the small woman at the front desk commented.

"Oh, that's okay. I don't want to go through."

"Then what are you here for?" Her expression went from puzzled to annoyed. She glanced at the clock and I could tell she didn't want me keeping her late.

"I was just wondering if by chance someone had left a message here for me."

"Are you Lina Pawlak?" She lifted out a folded piece of paper from her top drawer.

My heart thumped. "Yes. Really?"

"Yes, really," she repeated, handing me the paper.

I grabbed it out of her stubby hands.

Lina, I met you in another reality. You didn't know who I was. I tried to help, but Special Force was overpowering. It ended really badly. You need to be careful. Special Force is keeping tabs on you. Yusef

"You are quite a few hours late for your date," the woman chastised.

"He didn't look deserving of a stand-up."

I didn't have time to argue with her so I let her think I was a jerk.

"Show me Yusef Hassam."

His picture emerged.

Yusef Hassam, Status: Transition.

The woman turned to me, "What did you say?" She looked at my glasses. "Wow, how did you get those lights in your glasses?"

"It's just a trick." I sloughed her off while I scribbled a note on the back of his message.

Yusef, I've been here. Getting everybody out. Merging is dangerous. Please avoid. Love, Lina.

I shoved it back in the envelope and wrote his name on the front. "Can you please give this to Yusef Hassam?"

"I'm not a message service," she snapped.

"But Yusef needs you to be."

She let out a sigh. "Fine, whatever." She took the envelope and tossed it in the top drawer.

I had to find a private place to shift so I headed for the bathrooms.

Chapter 16

Back in the motel room, I paced the floor. I hadn't expected Jan to get back before me, but waiting for her was agony. I ate the sub in my backpack, and turned on the TV. The picture was bad, and the static was so loud I could barely hear anything, so I turned it off. Jan's phone rang. It was her parents. I didn't answer it.

I wanted to call Yusef. My need to talk to him was building. I looked at the phone and sighed. I would have to find another phone. I left a note to Jan, in case she came back. I grabbed my water bottle and key card and walked downstairs.

The sun had set. The late hour did the opposite of deter people from the avenue. Instead, the night owls flocked to the pubs and restaurants. Around the corner of the building, I saw a small newspaper shop and ducked inside. It was busy. The customers were browsing the shelves and talking. The clerk was facing the back shelves, pulling down packs of cigarettes.

"Excuse me. May I borrow your phone?"

Thirsty, I took a sip of water. When the clerk turned around, I took one look at him and spat the water out of my mouth. His front teeth were missing. It was the same clerk from the Wild West. Mr. Aims.

I regained my composure. "Sorry." I wiped my face and the counter with the sleeve of my hoodie.

Mr. Aims's expression was stale. He handed the smokes to an old man and rang them in. Then he turned to me. "You say you wanted a phone, missy?"

"Please," I said from behind my sleeve.

He handed me a cordless and I thanked him. I plugged my ear

against the noise in the shop and rang Yusef's number.

"Hello?" I said when someone answered.

"Lina?" Yusef said. "What are you doing? I told you not to call."

"You just said not to use Jan's phone."

"How am I supposed to tell a convincing story if you aren't really kidnapped? Where are you? Are you out in public? Shoot, Lina, you can't let people see you."

"I'm sorry. I just wanted to talk to you."

"Why? Why, after like, five years of nothing you throw all this at me? Why do you want to be my friend again all of a sudden?"

"I've always been your friend," I whimpered, "and I miss you."

He sighed into the receiver. "You have to go. Go tie yourself up somewhere and wait for the cops to find you."

"Okay." I clung to the phone with both hands. "When this is all over, can we hang out again?"

"Aren't you dating your swim coach?"

"You know about that?"

"Everybody knows. It's a total scandal."

"Well, it doesn't matter."

"If you say so."

"Bye, Yusef."

"Bye."

I stood there holding the phone for a minute. A small TV sat on a cabinet behind the counter. The news was on, but the sound was off. I gasped when the screen changed to a picture of me. Underneath, it read *MISSING.*

Just like Spencer's posters.

Fear gripped me. Had I compromised Yusef's plan? My eyes flashed to the other wall where a video camera was recording my every move. Dang it. I yanked my hood over my head. It almost covered my eyes. Had anyone noticed?

I clumsily dropped the phone onto the counter. "Thanks, Mr. Aims."

"How'd you know my name?" He peered at me.

My already thumping heart pounded harder in my chest. "Um, your name tag." My voice was that of a scared child.

His eyes narrowed in suspicion. As he picked up the phone, I slipped out of the store as quietly as possible.

By the time I got back, it was close to midnight. I thought of having a shower, but figured my story would be more believable if I was grimy. I wanted to stay up and wait for Jan, but my body wouldn't let me. I fell onto the uncomfortable bed and crashed.

"Lina." Someone shook me hard. It was Jan. She was trembling and sweating. Her black hair matted to her forehead.

I bolted out of the bed. "Sorry, I fell asleep."

"Where's Glynis? I had her with me." Her voice was on the verge of cracking.

"You found her? What happened?"

"It was black. Everything was black. I thought something had gone wrong. You know, like I hadn't shifted properly. Like I was stuck in some sort of limbo."

She was shaking so badly, I pulled the thin blanket off the bed and wrapped it around her.

"But then Glynis touched me. I freaked out. We were in a prison." She shook her head. "No, it was more like a dungeon. I couldn't see two inches in front of my face. She thought I was going crazy because I didn't remember any of it."

"Were you still on school grounds?"

"I have no idea where we were, I don't even know what Glynis looks like. I couldn't see her face." She began to cry. "I tried to explain to her about the different realities. She didn't believe me."

"What about Torvald? Was he there?"

"Torvald? Yeah, he was there." She sniffed. "He's the one that tried to...to make her stay."

I put my arm around her. "Calm down and tell me what happened."

She sucked in a shaky breath. "I told her I'd come from a different reality and merged with myself. That's why I couldn't remember anything. I told her how the computer plugs got scanned. I showed her the plug and asked her to come back with me."

"Did she?"

"At first she wouldn't because Torvald was telling her not to. They had been there for five days. Their food came in a basket, lowered down from a hole in the ceiling. And there was a hole in the floor for, you know, to do your business. The smell was putrid. This motel room is paradise compared to that. Shifting was the only way out of there."

"So what was Torvald's problem? Why wouldn't he believe you?"

"Oh, he did believe me. He just wouldn't do it. Then Glynis wouldn't either 'cause she couldn't leave him." She paced the room. "I don't even know these people. They are so stubborn. I can't believe we're friends with them."

"We are. Best friends. Keep going."

"Torvald said he didn't want to risk the complications of merging. He didn't want to screw up his brain. He told Glynis she'd just have to come visit him. She told him he'd never get out of prison. They fought a lot. Finally she got fed up with him and came with me."

"But where is she?" I gasped and smacked my forehead. "I am so stupid. If she doesn't have an alternate, then she'll merge at the same location she was at before. She's still in the prison—or whatever is in its place."

I was so stupid. How did I not realize that before? I was never going to grasp the concept of navigating through realities.

Jan's phone rang. We both jumped.

"You answer it. I'm not with you." I handed it to her.

"Hello?" Jan listened for a minute, then her eyebrows arched. "What? How did you get there? We thought you were stuck in the prison."

Glynis.

Jan squealed and passed me the phone. "You were wrong. Glynis *does* exist here."

Relief flooded through me. "Where is she?"

"Australia."

"This is the freakiest thing I ever done." Glynis was hysterical. "My eyes are hurting so bad. It is so bright compared to all those days in darkness."

"How did you get there?" I interrupted.

"I'm in my grandparent's house in Melbourne. I asked my parents why we were back here and they said we live here. So I asked when we were going back to Canada and they said they've never been to Canada. My family never emigrated."

"That makes complete sense, that's why you weren't in any of my alternate memories. That's why Jan doesn't know you."

"Complete sense? This doesn't make any sense. How am I supposed to get back there? I need to find Torvald," she gasped. "How can we be hooked up now? He doesn't even know me does he? Why didn't Jan tell me?"

"How was I supposed to know?" Jan had her ear up to the phone, listening.

"Okay, okay. We need to get you here. You can snag him all over again. Then maybe you can convince his alternate to merge and get him out of that dungeon."

"Leave it to me, mates," Glynis said. "I'll figure something out. I'll call you in a day or two. Hopefully I can get to Torvald in time. Try to find him and prep him for me."

I laughed. "What exactly do you expect us to do?"

"I'm sure you'll think of something. I gotta go."

"Good luck, babe." Jan hung up the phone. She turned to me. "Did I just call her *babe*?"

"You do all the time. Welcome to merge-land." I chewed my lip. "So...what do we do?"

"I could buy her a ticket with the credit card."

"No, something seems wrong with that idea." I tried to think. "The last time you used it was to book this room, but you can't be connected to me. I've been kidnapped. You need to report it stolen or something."

Jan put her hands on her hips. "What are we going to do about you?"

I was pacing the floor. "Yusef said to tie myself up and wait for the cops to find me. If you say your card was stolen, they'll trace it to this motel. You've got to go back and act like you weren't part of this. It's four o'clock. You can get back before anyone wakes up." I pulled the sheet off the bed and twisted it up. "Here, tie me up with this."

Jan didn't hesitate. She looped the sheet around the bed frame and bound me tight. My shoulders bent so far back they felt like they would pop out of their sockets.

"Ouch."

"Sorry Lina, but this has to look realistic."

"Well since you're hogging all the fun," I grumbled, "you also have to hit me, knock me out."

She looked in my eyes. "This better work." She gagged my mouth with my towel and bathing suit from my backpack.

The last thing I remember was seeing her boot in my face.

Chapter 17

I awoke by the loud bang of bursting locks. Sunlight was pouring in the window. It took me a moment to register the throbbing pain on my face. I groaned. Someone crouched beside me, pulled my eyelids open and shone a flashlight into my pupils.

"Don't." I tried to yell, but the gag was in my mouth. I jerked away. The bed frame held me fast. The movement sent a pounding pain up to my skull.

"It's alright, Halina. It's all over. I'm Constable Perry with the city police. You're safe."

I focused past the light to the uniformed man crouching beside me and swept my eyes around the room. The movement really hurt. Other cops rushed in, guns raised. The officer slowly pulled the gag out of my mouth. It was covered in spit and blood.

"He...he's coming back," I stuttered. My jaw wouldn't work.

"Who is? Who did this to you?" He cut me loose from the sheets and I winced as pain jabbed into my shoulders.

"I don't know." I started crying. I could feel caked blood on my nose and a nasty bump on the back of my head. What did Jan do to me?

"Can you remember what happened?"

"No." I knew I had to be careful before I started spewing out stories.

"I can see shards of glass in your hair. Do you know how it got there? What's the last thing you recall?"

"I was at the pool. I was gonna leave a message for Coach Tyler. Someone came up behind me."

The paramedics came in with a gurney. The cop turned to them, "Notify her parents. Get her to the hospital. Her nose is broken. Check for signs of sexual assault."

"Can you move?" a woman asked me. I tried to lift my arms, but it felt as if they were dead. They lifted me onto the gurney and placed an oxygen mask over my face. They put a blanket over me. I realized I was in my underwear. Before they wheeled me out, I saw another officer come out of the bathroom.

I heard him say, "We found the credit card and one key card in the toilet. No prints."

Then I closed my eyes and sighed. All this, just to cover up for breaking a piece of glass, I thought. Actually, I knew it was to cover up a heck of a lot more than that.

When we got to the hospital, my parents were in the waiting room. They rushed over.

"Halina. Oh, Gerald, there's so much blood." My mom was bawling. Her curly hair fell in her face while she wiped her eyes with a soaked tissue, her brown overcoat draped over one arm. My dad wore a wrinkled grey suit with his shirt un-tucked. His tie hung loose around his neck.

Seeing them made me cry. Not just to pump up my story, but because I missed them. I could see the grief in their red eyes and I was the cause of it. It had been so long since I'd seen them—so long since I'd talked to them. I remembered yelling into the phone for help while my psycho school principal was barging into my dorm room. Here I was causing so much trouble and my family was suffering because of it. I was tired of fighting. I was tired of feeling alone. When Mom came to my side, I raised my arm—though painful—and I clutched the edge of her coat.

"We need to take her to emergency surgery," the EMT explained as she pushed me down the hall.

"Are you okay? Did he hurt you, honey?" My dad hovered over my face, the wrinkles in his forehead deeply pronounced.

Wasn't my broken nose obvious enough?

"I mean, did he rape you?" he mumbled.

"No, I wasn't raped." I tried to pull the oxygen mask off, but one of the many nurses surrounding me put it back on.

Mom burst into fresh tears. "Oh thank goodness. Oh, Halina, we were so worried."

Another nurse gently pushed my parents back. "She needs her nose fixed. You'll have to wait out in the lobby."

My parents gave me a worried look.

"I'll be fine," I said through the mask.

"We love you, baby." Mom let go of the gurney and held the tissue to her face. Dad put his arm around her shoulder. The doors closed.

I didn't let them do a rape kit. I was still a virgin, thank you very much. After the X-rays, the IV, and thousands of photos, they took swabs of the dried blood on my face. I felt like I was in an episode of CSI. Right before I went under for surgery, I remembered something. The glasses. Where were my RAS glasses? I was already too drugged to ask.

"Finally, you're awake." A nurse checked my IV. "I'll let your family know."

I tried to sit up. I was too dizzy. I touched my nose. It felt swollen like a puffball and there was tape across it. A low ponytail held back my tangled hair. I probably looked hideous.

"Hello, Halina. How are you feeling?" Instead of my parents, Constable Perry stood in the doorway. His starched, blue uniform jingled and clicked from all the gear attached to him—handcuffs, radio and gun.

I shivered. "What do you expect?" It came out more abrupt than I had wanted. The man had found me, rescued me from some imaginary captor. I changed my tone. "Sorry, I shouldn't act like that. I am really thankful for all your help."

He smiled and nodded. "You have every right to be on your guard. There is a trauma counsellor I would like you to speak with. I gave her card to your folks. I have a couple questions for you, but before I ask, I want you to know that we found your abductor and we have him in custody."

My jaw dropped to the floor. "What—how? I mean, how did you find him so fast?" I pushed on my chest as though I could stop my heart from hurting, as though I could slow it down.

"We questioned some of your friends at school and they noticed some suspicious activity. It didn't take long to track him down. We picked him up this morning. Of course, you'll need to fill in some details so we know exactly what to charge him with."

How could I charge someone for a crime they didn't commit? I didn't want to ask, but I had to know. "Who is it?" I prayed that he wouldn't say Yusef. Yusef wouldn't be so stupid as to frame himself.

"Gerome Tyler."

I gasped.

"I know. It's hard to accept when someone who is close to you turns out to be a criminal. Apparently, he was leading a double life. He has a wife and kid nobody knew about."

What was going on? My brain was on overload. "I didn't know. I should have sensed something was wrong. I was his girlfriend." Tears filled my vision.

This was all so screwed up. I really shouldn't have felt so cheated.

Gerome had already lied to me about so many other things. My world was upside down because of him.

"I want to see my parents."

Perry nodded. "That's perfectly understandable. I'll come back a bit later." He left the room.

Chapter 18

"Oh, my goodness." Jan jumped to her feet when I entered the dorm. I still hadn't looked in a mirror.

"Don't touch me," I said when she tried to hug me. "You are...so dead. One of these days I'm gonna break *your* nose."

"Hey, don't get mad at me. I made it look real. I did a good job."

"Here, let me give you a pat on the back." I picked up the chair at my desk. "I'm getting good at throwing chairs."

She backed up. "Ha, funny, Lina. Now put it down."

I dropped the chair. "I'm not really mad. You are a very convincing kidnapper, but how did they figure Gerome did it?"

She came and held my shoulders, careful not to hurt me. "Yusef might have planted the idea in their heads. I'm sorry. I know how smitten you were with him."

"I'm kind of past that, but still, he shouldn't get sent to jail for something he didn't do. What about his wife and kid?"

"Oh, Yusef made that up too. It just made sense since Coach Tyler disappears three days out of the week."

Oh, good. That toned down my broken heart a bit. "Tell me you've got my glasses."

"I gave them to Yusef. He was awestruck. He wanted to study them."

"I need to talk to that boy. Come on."

As we walked across the lawn to the boys dormitory, everyone we ran into gasped and asked, "What happened?" and "How are you feeling?" *Yada, yada, yada.* They also had to make some comment about Gerome. "I never trusted him" or "He is such a creep." Poor guy. Nobody was on his side.

"Did you talk to Torvald?" I asked as we went up the stairs.

"Yeah. Well, I mean I tried. He is a very large, very scary guy," Jan answered.

"He can appear intimidating at first."

"I spent eight hours in a dark dungeon with him." Jan stopped on the last stair, her eyes out of focus, staring at nothing. A guy kicked a soccer ball down the hallway, but she looked right past him.

"You okay?" I asked.

She zoned in again. "I just had an alternate memory of him making out with some blond chick in our bathroom. Glynis. When did this happen?"

"It happens all the time," I told her, pulling her up the last stair. "Good to have the old you back."

I knocked on Yusef's door.

"Come in."

The room was a disaster. Piles of paper surrounded three computers on Yusef's desk and two on his brother's. Electronic parts, dirty clothes, weights and garbage littered the floor.

Yusef and Ibram sat together, hunched over a pair of RAS glasses.

When Ibram looked at me, he did a double take. "What's up with you?"

"Don't ask."

"You," Jan said. "You snuck us into that rave." She gaped at me. "We really went to that?"

"What's up with her?" Ibram said.

"Don't ask." I repeated.

Yusef was staring at me the whole time. I couldn't read his expression. He was probably in shock from the sight of my face.

I finally broke the silence. "So why did you have to get my boyfriend locked up?"

"I knew you'd blame me for that. I just told them you were dating him and they came to their own conclusions. Besides, he was too old for you."

"Do I detect a hint of jealousy?" I smirked, followed by an awkward pause.

He changed the subject. "What I want to know is where you got these?" He held up the glasses.

"If I tell you, it might change your life forever."

No one responded. The Hassam boys just looked at me, their black eyes bottomless pits.

"What'll it be?" I asked.

Yusef blinked. "If you haven't noticed, our lives revolve around computers, but this is like—"

"Nothing you've ever seen before?" I finished his sentence. "Yeah, you've said that before."

"What?"

"In another reality, sport."

If an Indian could go pale, Yusef would have.

"Come on, I'm dying here." Ibram waved his hands in the air. "Go on."

"Okay, put the glasses on."

Yusef obeyed.

"Show me Halina Pawlak."

The lights started flashing and the fun began. The boys freaked out, gasping and grabbing their hair. They laughed. They cried. Even Jan looked impressed.

Yusef studied the words in front of his eyes. "Shifter. What does *that* mean?"

"It means I've traveled from one reality to another."

"Well, hook us up, sis." Ibram stood up and put his jacket on. "Teleport me. I'm ready."

I smirked. "It's not that easy. You can't just rush into this. If there is one thing I've learned, it's this, Shifting can cause *huge* problems."

He pouted like a little kid. "So, does that explain what happened to your face?"

"Ha. You have no idea."

Chapter 19

"Hey, honey, back for another taste? If you didn't get enough the first time, my offer to hook-up with you still stands." Torvald was lifting weights and kissing his biceps with every rep. The weight room was humid and stinky. The volume on his iPod was so loud we could hear the hard beats from across the room. He pulled out his ear buds. "As a warning, I'll let you know those black eyes of yours are a bit of a turnoff."

I laughed. It was amusing being on the butt end of his jokes. "This situation is a bit unfair for you since I know you, but you don't know me. I'll tell you again, I'm not the person you should be flirting with. Fortunately for you, I have someone here who will be more than willing to take you up on your offer."

He sat up and towelled off his forehead. "She better be a heck of a lot prettier than—" He froze when Glynis appeared. He held the towel over his mouth and took a small bite of it.

I started to laugh, but Jan smacked me. It was priceless seeing Torvald's protective walls just disintegrate in front of him.

After her long flight, Glynis had spent a good two hours covering up her exhaustion with perfect makeup and a messy hairdo. Not girly or cute, but sensuous and devilish. Her clothes were emo-gypsy. Today was her ultimate flirt challenge and that huge smile on her face showed just how much she enjoyed it. She knew what he liked even more than he knew himself.

Glynis sauntered up to him. "Well, Popcorn, I'd say you're even more buff than I remember."

Torvald regained his power of speech. "Am I supposed to know you? 'Cause I can see that introductions would be mutually beneficial."

Glynis laughed. "It's almost like he's got amnesia or something, Lina. It's gonna be sweet to hook him all over again. You've got to give me some fun time before we shift him."

I shook my head and sighed. "I'll leave you to it then."

"Take your time, babe," Jan said as we headed for the door.

I took one last peek. Glynis held out her hand and Torvald kissed it. How chivalrous.

An hour later, they came into the cafeteria. Yusef and Ibram were throwing commands at the RAS glasses, impressed with every result. I was helping Jan reinstall her memories.

"Remember the time we stayed up all night and went to school the next day, and you fell asleep in gym class while you were doing push-ups?"

"Ha. Yeah, but I've got two memories of the same day. In this reality, Glynis wasn't there and we only stayed up until four. I didn't fall asleep doing push-ups and I did more than you."

"No way," I said.

"You know it. You remember."

"Well, of course you can do more than me," I said with a huff. "You weigh less, so you can't lift as much."

"Excuses, excuses." She laughed and flipped her hair over her shoulders.

Yusef joined our conversation, "You know that thing about humans only using twenty-five percent of their brain?"

"Yeah."

"Well, if you both have double memories of most of your lives, then maybe you're using more than twenty-five percent. Not that it would make you any smarter. It's just your long-term memory is doubled."

"It does make us smarter," Jan argued. "I've done all my classes twice. If one of me forgets an answer or two, the other me will remember it."

"Perhaps, but how many times can you merge until you're brain capacity gets used up. Then what?"

"Ten times," I said. "Carmen, this girl I met, said the more you merge, the more your brain can't handle it. You'll go crazy—burst. But that's not the only reason that merging is a bad idea. You'll have ten sets of parents without a son. Ten Torvalds without a Glynis."

Jan laughed. "Ten Canadas without Jan Kurauchi as Prime Minister."

I frowned. "You might think that's funny, but there could be serious repercussions."

"So, how many realities are there?" Ibram asked.

"Thousands." I went into my backpack and pulled out a handful of plugs.

Ibram picked one up and turned it over in his hand. "And there is a new me in every one of them?"

"No. There are probably some realities you could shift to without merging. There are realities where we—as in this group of people—don't exist. Like, we were never born there. You can shift there and back without anything going wrong. In fact, I'm supposed to take you all to Carmen's reality so you can donate samples of your DNA."

"Awesome." Ibram put his coat on again. "Let's go."

"Not now. When I left, their vessel was under attack. I've got to make sure it's safe first."

"Something would change." Yusef pointed to the glasses. "My status would change. I would no longer be stationary. I'd be a shifter."

"Yusef," I leaned toward him, "one of you already is a shifter. If he comes here, you will automatically merge with him. I should have warned you sooner. I don't know when he's coming. I don't even know where he is."

"Then, in that reality, I would be missing a brother." Ibram took off his coat and sat back down.

"In that reality, Yusef is already missing," I told him.

Ibram took a moment to mull over my words. "This is complicated."

"That reality is called Big Brother. Jan, Glynis and I have all shifted out of there. There is this splinter-government-cult called Special Force. They monitored our every move. They were weeding out *undesirable* people and sending them to Exile."

"Why would they do that?" he asked.

"They're trying to create a superior race. But we got in their way. If we go back there they'll throw us in prison or send us to Exile, like they did with Spencer." I glanced over to Spencer's table.

"I get it. Spencer is so definitely undesirable." Ibram snickered.

"That's not funny," I chastised.

"What's not funny?" Spencer asked. He walked up to us and bent over, leaning his elbows on our table.

"The world is a mess," Yusef stated. He gave me one of those mysterious faces—the ones I couldn't interpret.

"Tell me something I don't know," Spencer said.

I could tell him *so* many things he didn't know. I could tell him his mother never had any confidence in him. I could tell him that if he got expelled she would assume he ran away, or killed himself. I could even tell him he'd been cloned over a thousand times and I'd met one of them.

That was when Glynis and Torvald entered the cafeteria. They were holding hands, but Glynis didn't look very happy.

"So, is everything on the up and up?" Jan asked.

"No. It's not," Glynis said. She sat down with a thump, and Torvald pushed in her chair.

He sat down beside her. "I'm here, aren't I?"

"Kind of. You're also stuck in a pitch-black prison with only one hope of escape."

"Don't you believe her?" I asked.

"I didn't at first. But then she started telling me things about me that she shouldn't have known. Things that *nobody* should know." He blushed a little bit. "That got to me."

"Are you ready to break out of prison?" I asked.

"No. I'm not going to do it." He clasped his hands behind his head. "I'll explain to you why. Because I don't want to mess with it. If there are two realities, there should be two of me."

"Funny," Jan said, "I spent hours trying to convince your alternate to merge and he wouldn't either."

"What? Seems like my new girlfriend forgot to mention that part. I should have known I was being tricked. Just goes to show, you can't trust women."

His walls were building back up. I had to gain his trust before it was too late. For Glynis's sake. She looked miserable.

"How do you expect to get your alternate out of that hole?" I said.

"I'll figure something out."

"You could send him a plug to one of those realities where he doesn't exist," Yusef suggested. "Then he would escape without merging. At least he'd be free."

"Where I don't exist? What kind of a place would that be? I'd rather take my chances in jail."

"Tor, come on." Glynis tugged on his shirt. "Do it for me."

His eyes softened for a moment. "Listen, hon, you have me. But if my alternate didn't want to come, I think you need to respect his decision."

"If Glynis can't convince you, I doubt any of the rest of us can," Yusef said.

Jan sighed. "I agree. Especially because now, I think there may be some legalities involved. *The Charter of Rights and Freedoms* might have a clause about forcing someone into a decision."

"Oh yeah, I know it," I said. "It says, and I quote, 'Thou shalt not force any man or woman to merge with any of the said person's alternates.'"

"That sounds like one of the eleven commandments," Jan said. "My alternate didn't have a choice. Nobody asked the Glynis in Australia if she wanted to merge. Why are we so hesitant?"

I let out a frustrated huff. "You know what? I don't need permission. I could shift you all right now just by touching you."

Torvald stood up and backed away from me.

"Calm down," I said with a sigh. "I'm not going to. Jan, Glynis and I made our decisions and I am going to assume that our alternates would have made the same decision. If you and your alternate have decided to be stationary, then I'll respect that decision."

"Well, I'll just find another Torvald and get him to merge." Glynis pouted.

"It won't matter how many you find. Torvald will make the same decision no matter what reality you find him in. You can force him if you want to, but he won't be very happy with you. In fact, it might ruin your relationship."

Glynis looked into Torvald's eyes and sighed. "I just can't sit around knowing you are stuck in that nightmarish catacomb. Lina, give me the old plug and let me take him something, like food and a blanket."

I nodded. "Let's go back to the dorms."

After Glynis had procured some supplies, we all squished ourselves into the tiny room. The sun had set and most of the students were going to bed. I closed and locked the door.

"Just make sure nobody is touching you," I warned.

She stood on my bed and everyone else squished onto Jan's. Torvald was practically in the bathroom. I gave Glynis instructions on how to use the glasses. When she disappeared, Ibram and Yusef squealed and grabbed their hair again. Torvald got so pale, I thought he was going to faint.

"It never gets old," Jan commented about the boys' reactions.

"How long till she'll shift back?" Torvald asked.

"Dunno. I guess it depends on what she wants to do with you," I answered.

He blushed. "Ha, very funny."

Only ten seconds later, Glynis appeared. She sat down on my bed with the food and blanket still in her hands. Tears filled her eyes.

"What happened?" Torvald approached her.

She looked up. "You weren't there, mate. You were gone."

"What does that mean?" he asked.

"I don't know. How would I know?" She turned to me. "Would they let him go?"

"Not very likely."

"Would they...kill him?" Her eyes moistened up again.

"No, I don't think so."

"Then what? Where is he?"

All eyes were on me. "They probably put him in Exile."

"What the heck is that?" Torvald asked.

"It's where they put undesirables." I reached over and removed Glynis's glasses. Knowing her habitual recklessness, I had a feeling she would try to shift to Exile and save him, but I couldn't let her. Not until I knew what was there. It was for her protection. I needed information which meant having a talk—with someone who was currently in a holding cell at the police station.

Chapter 20

Glynis had to bunk down with us, since she didn't have a dorm room. I couldn't leave the glasses and plugs in our room in case she tried to use them in the middle of the night. I thought about entrusting them to Torvald, but something made me feel uneasy about it—as if he wasn't going to give them back. Yusef and Ibram were anxious to shift, but without an imprint, they were unable. Ibram was a bit high-strung, which made Yusef my best bet.

"Yusef, I trust you." I waited until we were alone, then slipped him a shoebox where I'd put the glasses and the plugs. "Don't show your brother that you have these."

"Why not? If he wants to shift, then probably all of his alternates want to—you said so yourself."

"It's not that simple. You and I, I mean your alternate and I, we were careless. It got us into a lot of trouble with the Special Force. If we run into them again, they could kill us. We've got to be careful where we go. That's why I'm hoping your alternate will find a way here and merge with you so we don't have to go looking for him. Then we stay here and lay low."

"I don't like that idea, Lina. The Special Force already knows about this place and it won't be long before they take over. Then what? We just keep running and hiding?"

"I'll think about that when the time comes. First, we wait for your alternate. Then we save Torvald from Exile."

"Hmm. Well, what if my alternate never comes? What if he's already dead?"

Blood drained from my face. I hadn't thought of that. I was so preoccupied with my fake kidnapping, merging Glynis and Jan and now dealing with Torvald's stubbornness, I just assumed Yusef was taking care of himself.

"This is too much to think about. My brain is fried. We'll talk about this in the morning."

We stood there for a moment in awkward silence, until he turned and walked away.

When I went to get ready for bed, I looked in the bathroom mirror to study my face. It was the first time I had taken a good look at it. I looked miserable. My eyes were swollen and as purple as a plum. I didn't even recognize my nose. In fact, it looked like my father's big red nose on my face in its place. I had an old-man nose and plums for eyes. Flames of revenge licked inside my head, but what could I do? I wasn't about to kick Jan in the face. The flames had no fuel to keep burning. At least she didn't kick me in the teeth.

That night I awoke from the sound of my backpack zipper opening. *Dang it Glynis*, I thought. She was trying to find the plugs. I pretended to sleep and let her look. Catching her in the act would only make her ashamed and make Torvald angry. Besides, she wasn't going to find them in there anyways.

I cracked my eyelids open to see how she would react when she didn't find any plugs. I was sleeping on the floor since I had given her my bed. I could see her silhouette against the moon shining through the window. The silhouette was an odd shape. I opened my eyes a bit further. Maybe it was the way she was standing, but it looked like she had cut off all of her hair. She was taller, more masculine...

A wave of panic swept over me and I tilted my head up. Who was in my room? I checked the beds, and both the girls were there, sound asleep. I looked back at the intruder, trying to determine how I could protect us. Jan was the only one who still had a cell phone and it was on her nightstand. Glynis had a nail file on the bathroom counter. That would have to do. If I was fast enough, I could reach it before I got caught.

I looked at the intruder to see if he had noticed that I was awake. He set my backpack down. In his hand, he held a plug. How had I missed one? I was sure I had given them all to Yusef. Just as he turned, his eyes met mine.

Scrambling out of my blanket, I bolted for the bathroom. He came right behind me. I attempted to lock the door, but he already had his foot across the threshold. I slammed the door into his foot and he yelped.

Trying to hold the door closed, I fumbled in the darkness for the nail file, but my hands were shaking with adrenaline. He huffed as he banged on the door. My fingers hit the edge of the nail file and it plopped into the sink, out of reach. He was pushing the door and gaining ground. I wouldn't be able to hold it much longer, so I let go. He fell into the bathroom as I reached into the sink and grasped the nail file.

Both of us were panting, trying to catch our breath. He knew I couldn't go anywhere, so he took his time getting up.

I held the file like a dagger. "Don't come any closer."

"Lina."

He knew my name and I knew that voice. He flicked on the light and I gasped. Sandy-blond hair. Lips I had dared to kiss. It was Gerome. The file fell from my hands and clinked on the tile floor.

"What are you doing here?" My voice trembled.

"You had me locked up for something I didn't do." The anger in his voice was petrifying. He held up the plug. "You were going to leave me there, weren't you? You broke my heart. You're a liar and a fraud and that makes you an undesirable. I'm sending you to Exile."

He rushed at me, grabbing hold of my hair with his free hand. I screamed as he pushed me against the wall.

"Gerome. No."

He raised the plug to my neck, and everything went black.

I could feel Gerome's strong fingers still gripping my hair. The ground beneath us disappeared and we were falling. I screamed again, flailing my arms. A light rushed up toward us, dim at first, then growing brighter. Gerome pulled me to his face and kissed me, pushing against my mouth. I slapped him, but he was no longer Gerome. He was Yusef. The dim light beneath us became the bathroom tiles, with a hundred nail files pointing up at us. We were falling faster than gravity, as if the floor was sucking us down. I screamed and braced for impact.

My eyes flew open, and I examined my body for a hundred stab wounds, but found none. I was on the dorm room floor breathing hard with my blanket twisted around me in a knot. My forehead was damp with sweat.

Jan and Glynis were both sound asleep on either side of me.

I slowly exhaled and hung my head in my hands. It was hours before I fell asleep again.

Chapter 21

"Empty your pockets," Constable Perry requested.

I hadn't brought anything. I came alone. I convinced everyone else to go to their classes. I said we would figure this all out after school. I didn't tell anyone where I was going.

"Are you sure you want to do this?" the police officer asked.

"Yes, I'm sure," I answered.

He led me down a narrow hallway to a small room with a table and chairs.

"Wait here."

A moment later, he escorted Gerome Tyler into the room and sat him down across from me. I heard the clink of the handcuffs as he rested his arms on the table. His grey coveralls clashed against his bright skin tone. Pity overcame me.

He stared at me for a long time, studying my messed up face. He finally spoke with a raspy, unused voice. "Lina, how could you possibly believe I could ever do something like that to you?"

"I never said..." I paused, glancing up at Constable Perry. "I just want this to be over. I want to forget the whole thing."

Suddenly the whole kidnapping story was so stupid. I should have 'fessed up to breaking the window. They could charge me with vandalism and make me fix it. That would have been a slap on the hand compared to this. This was a royal mess with a broken nose and a boyfriend in custody.

"Are you willing to throw me in jail?" he asked. "I'll lose my job."

"You've already lost your job for dating one of your students," I replied.

"I'll never be able to come back to Safe Place again."

Perry gave him a sideways glance. Gerome ignored it. I had to ask him about Exile. I needed his help.

"That's not my problem," I mumbled, trying to keep a façade of vengefulness.

"Please, Lina. Tell them it wasn't me."

"Tell me what happened to Torvald? Is he in Exile? Can we get him out? Tell me why my friends were held hostage in some black pit. Tell me why you are involved with Special Force." I clenched my fists. "I want to help you, but you've got to help me." I was acting so tough, but Gerome still made me feel weak. He was so freaking gorgeous sitting there, taking everything I dished out. I wanted to jump over the table and smooch him.

Perry spoke up, "Is there something more to this?"

"Yeah, it's called blackmail," Gerome said.

"Halina, would you mind explaining this to me?" Perry asked.

"It's just a game," I bluffed. "A game that got taken way too far."

"And you are continuing to play this game with the man who abducted you? That is not why you came here today. We need to get a confession out of this guy or the whole thing is going to trial."

Gerome put his head in his hands. "I never meant to hurt her."

"But you did. Isn't that right, Tyler?" Perry asked.

"Yeah, okay, I hurt her. I betrayed her because I'm too chicken to stand up for her. I'm too chicken to fight against the Special Force. I'm even too chicken to see Exile. I don't know what it looks like. I don't know how to save those people."

"Enough with the games," Perry said.

Gerome kept going. "And you know what, Lina? I don't even want to. I wanted it to be you and me, cozy and safe. Forget about Big Brother. Forget about the Special Force. Just live our lives in this world that I found for you, but it wasn't good enough for you. Your little friends weren't cool enough, so you had to shift them here. Well, now the Special Force knows, and sooner or later they will find you and Exile you, and I won't be able to save you because I'll be stuck in here."

"Enough," Perry shouted. "You are done speaking with her." He pulled Gerome to his feet. "Halina, you stay here. I have some questions for you when I get back."

Gerome looked at me. "Lina, all I need is one plug—"

"So you can go back to Big Brother and tell them where I am?"

The hurt in his face was deep. "No. Lina, I would never."

I wanted to believe him so badly. I wanted to imagine him rescuing me from the fiery dragon and riding off into the sunset together. I wanted to get sucked into his beautiful eyes and stay there forever. I wanted to bust those handcuffs off him and disappear.

I watched, helpless, as Constable Perry pushed Gerome out the door.

I didn't stay. I had no idea how to explain myself to Perry, so I wasn't going to try, but before I left the building he caught up with me.

"Halina, I told you to wait for me."

"Sorry, I'm busy." I tried to continue toward the door, but he stood in front of me.

"You need to tell me what that was all about." He folded his arms across his chest.

"No, I don't."

"This is relevant to your case and you cannot withhold information."

"This has nothing to do with my case and I can withhold whatever I want." I tried to push past him. A couple other cops were approaching. They blocked the doorway.

"What is the Special Force?" he demanded.

I shrugged my shoulders. "It's a terrorist group from another reality that has taken over the government. They monitor our every move. They are trying to create a superior human race by weeding out the weak."

One of the other two cops smirked. "Where did you pick up this one, Perry?"

"Come on, this isn't a joke."

"I told you, it's a game."

Three uniforms scowled down at me. "Listen, I'm not devaluing everything you've done for me. I appreciate you finding me. I appreciate you catching Gerome. I just don't think it was him."

They scowled harder.

"If you're not going to allow me to talk with him again, then I want to leave."

Perry sighed. "Let her go."

"Thank you."

The officers stepped aside and I hurried past them.

Chapter 22

The late morning sun shone, though the outside air was frigid. I pulled my hands up into my sleeves. Frost floated out of my lungs and clung to my hair and the edges of my hood. As I walked back to the school, I thought about what Gerome had said. He wanted to hide away with me and forget about Big Brother's problems. He wanted to look the other way while the Special Force charged through the planet and scooped up anyone they didn't like. It was so immature—flattering to me—but unproductive to the rest of the world.

It was then I realized that I had not done anything either. I was so concerned with saving my friends that I had left the rest of the world to rot under Special Force's tyranny. I thought saving all of my friends was a noble cause, but really, I just wanted them with me to make *me* happy. I was being just as selfish as Gerome was.

The Special Force needed to be stopped, although I hadn't considered that I would help stop them. I just thought someone else would do it. A war was brewing, and I was ready to sit it out.

I had a chance to stay and fight on the Earth Station, but I didn't even consider it. I hadn't even brought them any new DNA like I had promised. I wondered what Carmen was doing right now? I wondered if she was even safe.

I felt lousy. I hadn't helped anyone except my friends and myself. This was no ordinary problem. It wasn't like trying to get good grades or competing for gold in the Summer Games. I never wanted to be ordinary. I wanted adventure, but I never pictured anything like this.

Now the adventure was serious. I couldn't play around in the pool when I knew people were drowning. I had to have the guts to dive in from the platform. If I were brave enough to go rescue Torvald from Exile, then why wouldn't I rescue everyone from Exile? Why wouldn't I save everyone from every reality?

If I hadn't been so preoccupied with my thoughts, I probably would have noticed them sooner—it was common to see a couple of Goths storming down the avenue—so, when I saw a group of tall, black cloaks a couple of blocks ahead of me it didn't register. It wasn't until I noticed they were heading toward the school that I realized who they were.

The Special Force. Arter's thugs. Probably the same four as before. I had no plugs with me and no glasses. I didn't even have a phone so I could warn my friends. Gerome's favourite cafe was just ahead and I ducked inside to think. Gerome was right. They had come for me. I was sure after two of my friends disappeared from their prison, they would know I had rescued them. After their swim coach didn't show up for work, of course they would come here looking for him. It was only a matter of time.

It was hopeless to hide. Besides, all of my friends were at the school. I couldn't let them get captured.

I slipped back onto the street, saying a small farewell to the cafe Gerome would never take me to again. The south entrance to YAC was still a block away. I would have to go to the north entrance and get there before them so I turned the corner and ran. My feet were heavy and I strained to keep up a fast pace. The chilly air stung my lungs as I tried to gather more oxygen. I pulled off my hood to avoid sweating.

I cut through the soccer field and jumped the fence, landing badly and twisting my ankle. My ears were aching. My eyes were stinging. I was gasping for breath. I bent over and tried to slow my breathing.

"Keep going."

I heard Gerome's words in my mind. It was force of habit, ingrained from hours of training, but it was also because I appreciated his coaching. He was right, and I listened to him.

I got back into a brisk jog. The fitness centre was the building closest to me, and the courtyard was next, then finally the dorms. When I got to the trees at the edge of the courtyard, I stopped. I could see them approaching from the other side of the cafeteria. As soon as I came out of my cover, they would see me. Could I outrun them? Probably not in my present state—I was already exhausted. I shook my head. I was so tired of hiding, but it was all I could do.

Crouching down, I watched as they approached the girls dorm. As they filed inside, I had a revelation. What I needed was not in my dorm room. As soon as the door closed, I bolted over to the next building—the boys dorm.

Instead of going in the door, I went around the side and climbed up to Yusef's window. The trellis shook as I barrelled up. Prying the window open, I slid over the sill and into his room. Finding the shoebox under his bed, I took out the glasses and left the rest of the plugs. If I was about to get caught, I didn't want them confiscated. I looked at the time, 11:54. The lunch hour was about to begin. I had to hurry before any of my friends showed up. I left my student ID as evidence that I had been there, then I ran out the door.

Just as I came outside, the four men in cloaks were leaving the girls dorm. They were about to split up and search the grounds.

"Hey," I yelled to them, "looking for me?"

"Halina Pawlak, do not try to run," one of the men called.

I didn't.

They approached me cautiously. "Throw down your weapons and all of your plugs."

"I don't have any." I raised my hands in surrender. "You better hurry before anyone sees you."

The men had puzzled expressions. "Y'all are willing to come with us?" one asked. I recognized him as Hill-Billy, the henchman from the Wild West.

I didn't answer.

"I'll take that as a yes." He searched my pockets, but found nothing. "Alrighty, boys, let's take 'er in."

The four men placed one hand on each other's shoulders and the other hand on mine. Hill-Billy raised a plug to his neck and we all disappeared.

Chapter 23

I was back in the clump of trees between the courtyard and the dorms. The sun was shining. A few students came outside and headed toward the cafeteria. I could see students in the ped-way. My face dropped. The ped-way had an extra high roof with space for another room above it. I was in Big Brother.

I was right back at the beginning—right where I had last shifted out of my home reality. I looked around and realized the henchmen hadn't shifted with me. Of course they hadn't. I could make a run for it. I could shift out of here, and they would never find me. I could keep myself safe, but how would I keep my friends safe? I shook my head. I already resolved not to be so selfish. Arter's henchmen would only come back for me. The thought that in order to keep my friends safe I might never be able to go back to Safe Place filled me with dread.

My choices were very limited. They narrowed even further when I heard someone yelling my name.

"Halina Pawlak. We know you are in the school grounds. Come to the courtyard immediately."

I peered through the trees at the courtyard. Four men clad in black were approaching. A fifth member had joined their entourage, although he wasn't there voluntarily.

It was Torvald. He was filthy. His matted hair stuck to his head. His eyes were red and bloodshot, his lips chapped, hands tied behind his back and snot ran from his nose.

Hill-Billy shoved him into the courtyard and sneered. "Miss Pawlak, y'all better show yourselves or this guy will be headin' off to Exile."

I ground my teeth. I couldn't escape. Maybe if I could get close enough to Torvald I could take him somewhere safe. Somewhere he wouldn't merge...

"Save yourself," Torvald yelled in a raspy voice.

One of the henchmen kicked him hard in the back of the legs and he collapsed to his knees on the concrete bricks of the courtyard. The man pulled out a gun and pointed it at the back of Torvald's head. "I think we should kill 'im instead," he growled.

How could they be doing this in a public place in the middle of the day? Had no one else noticed? I looked up at the ped-way and saw a couple of students staring out the window. Maybe I could signal them for help. A teacher came up behind them and shoved them into the flow of traffic toward the cafeteria. They obeyed without question. They were petrified. The grip of the Special Force had grown too strong. They must have increased their threats beyond expulsion from YAC. I imagined this display wasn't the first public viewing of their power. I shook my head. The school might be lost, but I knew others would fight. I thought of my friends, my parents and the police. I was not alone.

"You can't kill him." I found some courage and stepped out from my hiding spot. "You can't have blood on your hands. Your plan will never succeed if you resort to murder. Our parents will know, the police will find out. You can't kill everyone and you can't send them all to Exile." I leaned against one of the stone benches outlining the courtyard. "This ideal society the Special Force is trying to create will never work. Someone will always oppose you. You can try to take over the world, but eventually you'll lose. You'll all be put away like Saddam Hussein. You'll be brought to justice and hung up in a tree—all of you."

I was on the exact opposite side of the courtyard from Torvald. He was fifteen metres away from me. He looked up at me with pain in his eyes and gave a subtle shake of his head. The man behind him smacked him on the head with the butt of the gun and Torvald fell to the ground. Coughing, he rolled to one side and spat blood out of his mouth.

"We weren't gonna kill him." He raised the gun to point at me. "We just needed him as bait to find you."

"What for? What have I done to deserve all of this drama? You chase me everywhere I shift. For what purpose?"

"You're the kind of threat that must be crushed before you build up an army and try to oppose us."

"I'm not building up an army. I just want to get away from you." I balled my hands into fists.

"That's what all your alternates say," Hill-Billy said. "Then y'all fight back an' we gotta go to war. I don't want to have to blow up another planet to prove our superiority. We recruit the best DNA, the most polished, disciplined minds. We leave the irresponsible, immature, corrupted gene pool to you. Your lot is weaker. You'll catch diseases quicker and die off sooner. And good riddance. Y'all don't stand a chance against us."

"Then let Torvald go," I demanded. "You have me. I surrender."

"Ha. It ain't that simple. See, we want him to join Special Force. His DNA is pristine, as are most of you kids in this here school. We screened y'all before we even admitted you. But we couldn't predict yer attitude. We need willin' subjects, and this guy's attitude is unacceptable. We always give the defiants one last chance before we sentence them to Exile. 'Cause once yer there, there ain't no coming back."

Hill-Billy walked up to the crumpled body of Torvald and bent down. "So what'll it be, son? You ready to join the superior and the unstoppable? Or are y'all as stupid as you look?"

Torvald peered sideways at the men in black robes. Blood was congealing on his bottom lip. He coughed as he tried to talk.

"Speak up, sonny." A man kicked him in the back.

Maybe I could sneak closer while their attention was off me. I inched away from the bench into the middle of the courtyard.

Torvald cleared his throat and tried again. "First of all, you come into my school and started messing around with my privacy. You monitor my every move. You judge me, and you're unfair. Then you hold me hostage in a stinky, dark pit for six days. You torture me and threaten to kill me, and then you expect me to put on my happy face and support your Taliban-Darwin-Nazi-Satanic cause? I don't think so."

He spat at his captor and received a hard slap on the cheek.

I took a few steps closer.

"Lina, stay out of this," Torvald said. "Do what you can to get out. Tell Glynis I'm sorry."

"Come on boys. Let's Exile this defiant." They hooted as if this was a mob lynching.

"You better stay back, missy, or we'll throw one at you too." Hill-Billy pulled out a black plug from his cloak. He didn't need to tell me which reality it was for. The other three men also held out plugs. They backed away and each took a turn chucking their plug at Torvald, trying to hit the imprint on his neck.

"That was a close one."

Torvald rolled onto his stomach to avoid the plug. He pulled his shoulder up high, trying to cover up his imprint, but they just kicked him again. All it would take was one of those plugs hitting the right spot and Torvald would disappear. I cringed with every toss. Maybe I could move fast enough to grab him and shift out of there. Probably not before four grown men captured me. If I rushed in, I might touch Torvald right when a plug hit him. That would transport both of us to Exile. Still, I was not about to escape without him. Even if it was impossible to save him, I had to try.

I stepped closer. No one was watching me.

"Time to go to no-man's-land," one henchman yelled. He threw his plug and clocked Torvald on the forehead.

"You'll pay for this," Torvald yelled back.

"How do you expect to do that? Kick me? Punch me? Fight me? Where you're going you ain't gonna have no arms or legs." He laughed.

The next man was laughing so much his toss went wide. Torvald's eyes widened and he tried to scoot away. He backed into a stone bench and tried to roll under it. The men all picked up their plugs and tried to hit him again.

"Let's just make this easier and stop him from twitchin'." Hill-Billy had his back toward me. He smacked Torvald's forehead against the leg of the stone bench, knocking him out cold. They started throwing plugs again, this time taking careful aim.

I only had four metres left to close the gap. I held my breath.

The next toss flew through the air in slow motion. It headed straight for Torvald's neck and landed dead on the mark.

"No," I screamed, rushing toward him with all of my might. Too late. I watched him disappear. Besides a puddle of bloody spit, the spot of concrete under the bench showed no evidence the he had been lying there at all. It was as if he didn't even exist.

The four men turned to face me. Evil grins spread across their faces. I was standing close enough for a draft of their stench to reach my nostrils. With Torvald gone, their advantage against me was also gone.

"Come on now, missy, I believe the principal would like a word with you."

"No." I turned and ran. I got back to the trees before I was tripped by Hill-Billy's football tackle. I skidded to a stop in the grass. Two others came up and grabbed my arms, intending to drag me up. Just one more. They all had to be touching me in order to shift out of here and I had to do it before anyone knew where they had found me.

I kicked my legs hard. It was just enough of a struggle to warrant the fourth guy grabbing me.

"Shift me to Earth Station," I yelled in desperation.

They never knew what hit them.

Neither did I.

Chapter 24

It was cold—frozen with no ice. It wasn't the late November chill normally found in this part of Canada. It felt like being dunked in liquid nitrogen. My blood was freezing inside my veins. I was trying to swim and I couldn't break the surface. I *was* swimming, but with no friction and no momentum. I opened my eyes and instantly the surface of my pupils began to freeze. I squeezed them shut, but not before I realized what I was looking at. Blackness lay all around me—blackness with dots of light. Pieces of twisted metal and shattered glass were surrounding me, along with the complete absence of warmth. I was suspended in space floating among the wreckage of the Earth Station.

The tight grip of four strong men was gone. They were staring at me, mouths gaped open with no sound coming out. No atmosphere. No air to breathe. No way to move. In a matter of seconds, we would all be frozen to death.

I was desperate to shift out of there, but not before I made sure none of them were touching me. I had to open my eyes again. Lifting my eyelids just a crack, I found the closest body. It was Hill-Billy, and he was right under me, reaching for my leg. My body felt useless. With great effort, I kicked off from his chest and did a rolling somersault up and away from my captors.

"Take me to the..." I was moving my lips, but no sound was coming out. My lips were so cold I could no longer move them. My head was spinning. I was passing out from lack of oxygen and pure cold.

"Garden of Eden." My jaw sloshed through the silent words and I fainted.

Violent shaking. Searing pain in my limbs. Blood pushing inside me, like being forced through a potato masher. Eyes. My stinging eyes.

A blanket, hot and burning. Black windows. An IV. A pump. An oxygen mask.

Not another oxygen mask. I lifted my arm to remove it but I had limited control of my muscles. Someone clasped my arm and gently placed it back on the bed.

"I'm so sorry, Lina. The Special Force destroyed the Earth Station and we haven't had time to rebuild it." It was Carmen's voice. She patted my hand.

I knew she was sitting beside me, but my vision was clouded and blurry. I blinked a few times and it got a little better. I recognized her white and grey uniform.

"I'm afraid your friends didn't make it."

"My friends?" I whispered. "Those weren't my friends."

"Oh?"

"They were trying to kill me."

"You mean you left them there on purpose? Oh Lina. I just assumed you were trying to bring us fresh DNA."

I laughed in a quiet, wheezing sort of way. "I don't think you want clones of those guys."

"I suppose not."

"What happened?"

"Shelley-407 found you lying in the doorway of the hothouse. You were having a seizure. She alerted the medical centre right away. When I saw your profile on RAS, I came right away. You're the first person I know to float in outer space unprotected for eight seconds and survive."

"Lucky me. It's not so bad. Anyone could do it." I wheezed.

"Anyone out of their mind." She patted my hand again. "How do you feel?"

"Crappy." I tried to lift my arm again, this time it worked much better. I pulled off the oxygen mask. "I hate talking with these things on."

"Well, I see you still have your attitude, so you can't be in too bad of shape."

"Did everyone get out of the Station before..."

Carmen smiled a sad smile. "We had a few casualties. Captain Thomas opted to stay with his ship."

"Oh. That's too bad. I'm sorry to hear it."

"I am heading the operation to rebuild Earth Station. I'll be appointed captain when she's complete."

"Wow, that's amazing." I was almost callous with my lack of enthusiasm, but I had no energy to spare.

She stood up as a nurse walked in and checked my blood pressure. "I'll come back in a while to see you again."

"Thanks, Carmen."

The nurse spoke up. "Your blood pressure is very low. You need to rest." She added something to my IV and turned out the light.

I slept for twelve hours. When I woke up, I had to pee like a racehorse.

"At least I know my body still works," I muttered. My muscles ached. My bones ached. I felt like I was eighty years old. A familiar grey and white, ribbed jumpsuit was waiting for me. I was actually glad to put it on. I even tied my hair back.

"Show me the location of Carmen the First," I asked my glasses.

A map of the building popped up and showed a red dot in the mess hall. Oh good, I thought, I'm starving.

The building I was in was not unlike the space station in design. It appeared to be among the smaller buildings in the Garden of Eden horticultural colony. Instead of a spectacular view of the stars, the windows gave a view of orchards, fields and gardens. Even though they were dormant for the winter, I could imagine them full of sunny blossoms and ripening fruit. I could see people moving from building to building, hauling things out of storage sheds and onto large trucks. Another window revealed a huge construction project that I assumed would become the new Earth Station.

The mess hall was over crowded. It made me realize the survivors of the Station's destruction were taxing the colony. I saw multiples of the same faces—clones. People were staring at me as if I was the weird stranger.

"Lina," Carmen called. She was sitting at a table with two other women who were identical to her in every way. They all tilted their heads and smiled.

"I didn't know they had released her yet," one said.

"Oh, they haven't," another replied. "This is the original." Their voices were so similar it would have sounded like one person if I closed my eyes.

After eating, Carmen grabbed my hand. "Come with me, Lina, I want to show you something."

She led me to a separate building with a large mural of a string of DNA stretching across the outside wall. Inside I saw laboratories similar to the one that had been on the Station. The tubes filled with gooey phlegm hung mounted on the walls. The strange forms of adult bodies were stacked like mannequins behind a partition, waiting to come to life.

The forms inside the incubation chambers were indistinguishable through the clouded glass. The very end held an alcove with a number of hospital beds filled with patients attached to observation equipment. The patient in the last bed was getting her blood pressure checked. She had very short red hair.

"Lina, I would like to introduce you to your prototype clone."

The girl on the bed turned to look at me. "She's my clone?"

"No, you are hers," the nurse said and pulled the cuff off her arm.

We stared at each other. I'd never seen myself with short hair. My whole life I had let it grow. Something else looked different about her—it was her expression. She looked so innocent and eager to learn.

The nurse turned to me. "Sometimes it takes a while for the clones to realize who and what they are, but she is reacting the same way you would if I told you that you were a clone."

"Wow, I'd love to have hair like yours. Can you pull it down so I can see how long it is?"

"Sure." I let it out of the knot. "I've never seen my hair so short."

"She's only had a week to grow it," Carmen said.

The nurse pulled out an official-looking document. "She's ready to be released. Can you sign for her?"

Carmen pulled out a pen and signed her name. "I usually get the nurse to witness, but it's fitting that you do it since you're here. Some originals never get to meet their clones." She handed me the pen.

"Wow, thanks." I signed my name beside hers.

"Lina-2, we would like to take you to lunch before you have your orientation," Carmen requested.

My clone stood up and we walked together back to the mess hall.

"You're my height and build. I mean of course you are, but it's just so amazing," she said to me.

"Funny, I was about to say the same thing."

"Except for your nose."

"Ha, yeah."

"We could be best friends," she said.

"I'm good friends with quite a few of my clones. It's so easy to understand each other." Carmen held the door open for us as we stepped outside.

"Friends, yeah. I'd love to introduce you to my friends." It was the first time I'd thought about them since my near-death experience. I looked at Carmen. "I have some problems that I need your help with. Is there a way to rescue someone from Exile?"

"Tell me what happened." She sighed.

I told her about Gerome. I told her how the Special Force had found me. I told her about Torvald. My clone kept up with the conversation with peaked interest.

"How can someone get Exiled to a place that is impossible to shift back from?" she asked.

"Imagine shifting to a reality where things you are used to don't exist. They will morph into something else. Something that already exists in that reality."

"Like my phone becoming a horseshoe."

"Exactly. Now imagine a reality where human beings don't even exist. Your physical body has to morph into some other living creature. What would you become?"

I shook my head. "That couldn't happen. How could there be an earth without humans?"

Lina-2 spoke up. "Even if we turned into monkeys, we could still shift back."

"Imagine an earth that is entirely covered in water. There are no land-roving animals at all. It becomes very difficult to hold a plug with no opposable thumbs, let alone touch it to your neck. What if you have no neck?"

"Has anyone made it back?"

"Many have attempted a rescue mission and very few have come back. The problem has always been the same. They can't hold onto the plug. They tried strapping the plug to their arms, but they may lose their arms and end up as fish, or the strap disappears because it can't exist. It is dangerous because the physical body you assume is unpredictable. We've lost more people while attempting rescues than the people exiled in the first place. The missions were abandoned when we dissolved the act disallowing cloning."

"Good thing, or you wouldn't be here," Lina-2 said to me.

"No, *you* wouldn't be here," I corrected her.

"She'll catch on when Lina 3 and 4 are out of incubation," Carmen said.

"We can get them out of there," Lina 2 said.

"What do you mean?" Carmen asked. "They are still in incubation."

"No, I mean the Exiles."

"What? How?" She caught my interest. I thought of Torvald and Spencer.

"You have been trying to rescue humans, but they aren't humans. They're fish. How do you catch fish?"

"With a net." Carmen brightened. "Made out of some kind of material that exists under water."

"Seaweed," she said.

Carmen clapped her on the back. "Fresh brains bring fresh new ideas. I will start working on something right away." She left us sitting at the table and walked straight out of the mess hall.

Lina-2 turned to me. "Extra fresh brains." She tapped her forehead.

I laughed.

Chapter 25

"So, any object you shift with will automatically merge with itself if it exists in that new reality."

Yusef was drawing a chart on his whiteboard as the rest of us looked on. It felt like we were a bunch of students listening to Professor Hassam. Glynis, Jan, Torvald, my clone and I squished ourselves into Yusef's dorm. It was everyone in Safe Place who knew about the shifting secret, except Ibram, and I wasn't sure where he had gone.

Lina-2 was really enjoying herself. Yusef kept looking at her in disbelief. Carmen gave us permission to shift together to Safe Place. I needed to make sure my friends were all okay. So far, no one else from Special Force had shown up. I also wanted to show off Lina-2 a little bit. Yusef had been devising a scheme while I was gone.

"But, if the object *doesn't* exist, it will be transformed into something compatible with the reality. It will only exist if it is invented and built in that reality." He drew an O and connected it to an X from one section to another. "There is an exception. The plugs remain the same."

Jan joined in. "So it will be impossible to, say, shift electricity or a car or—"

"A phone," I interjected.

"Yes, exactly. You can't shift something to a place where it doesn't exist and try to make money off your great discovery."

"This process could work in reverse. If we wanted something to stop existing we would shift it into a reality where it didn't exist." Yusef drew an X changing to an O.

"That wouldn't work," Glynis said. "To get rid of a cell phone you'd have to get rid of all of the cell phones on earth and every person who knew how to build one."

"Point taken," Yusef said, "but what if we had only one of these objects? Once it is gone, it can't come back."

I thought for a moment. "You want to shift RAS itself."

"Yes. Once it is gone, its original state doesn't exist here anymore. My guess is it would become just a regular computer like any other with no advanced technology. Someone who knew how would have to rebuild it in secret, but we'll face that problem when it happens."

"You're brilliant." Lina-2 smiled.

"So, Lina-1, you must know a reality where RAS doesn't exist. Where do we take it?" Yusef asked.

"Exile," I answered. "Nothing exists there but ocean."

Silence enveloped the room as my words sunk in. In order to get RAS to Exile, someone would have to take it there. Everyone made a conscious effort not to look at Torvald. He hadn't said anything since I told him his alternate had been Exiled. I wondered if he doubted his decision not to merge. He could have saved himself if he had. Glynis hadn't said much to him either. She wasn't even sitting beside him.

"But Lina," my clone turned to me, "Carmen said nothing can get back. Who would voluntarily send themselves there?" I had told her to keep the idea about the net a secret. They didn't need to know.

"I would," I answered.

"No, Lina, you can't." Jan put her hand on my shoulder.

"Jan, you know how to get into Gerome's secret room. Don't go through the door. Use the broken window. You have to steal the computer and bring it back here. I'm going to Garden of Eden to tell Carmen my plan. She might be able to find a way to get me back. Lina-2, you need to stay here and go to my classes for me so I don't get kicked out of school."

"Everyone's gonna love your new do," she said, brushing her hand over her spikes.

I smiled at her, and she smiled back like a mirror. I hadn't heard her disagree with me once since the moment I met her.

Jan, on the other hand, was not so cooperative. "Lina, this is suicide. You told us what happened to Torvald. You told us other rescue attempts have failed. Why there? Why does it have to shift there?"

"Because, the Special Force won't ever find it. Listen, you guys do your job and I'll do mine." I had another reason for what I was doing, but I wasn't about to tell them. They thought I was enough of a martyr already. They might tie me up and never let me go.

"Lina." Jan stood up. "I merged here to escape from prison and be here with you. You are my best friend. What if you never come back? I mean, I don't want to sound selfish, but think about what you're doing to me."

I stood up too. "This reality is not going to be safe until we can find a way to banish the Special Force. We can't think of just our little clique anymore. Other people out there need our help. When I look around this room, I see it crammed full of my best friends. Some of you might not realize it," I looked at Yusef, "but you are. I've been doing everything I can to help you. On the way, I found someone named Carmen and she has a greater goal than just fighting to save herself. In her reality she has to fight to save everyone—every living soul. If we don't do something, Safe Place might fall to the same fate as Big Brother. Then what will be the point of sticking with our own?"

Yusef nodded. "You're right, Lina. We can't sit around and turn a blind eye to what is happening. You've seen Special Force get a dangerous grip of the country and even the world. We have to prevent that from happening here in Safe Place, or soon there will be nowhere safe to shift to."

I looked at Yusef and felt a rush of pride. "I knew you would say something like that."

Jan threw her hands up in the air in defeat. Glynis said nothing, but she glanced sideways at Torvald, a pained look on her face. He came over to her and put his arm around her.

I changed the subject. "So, where is Ibram?"

"Getting recruits." Yusef capped his pen.

"Recruits for what?" I asked.

"Recruits for the Unified Defenders."

"The what?"

"We thought about calling ourselves the Rebel Alliance, but that's been done before."

"You can't tell. I mean, this is supposed to be a secret," I argued.

"Why not?" he questioned. "How can we let the human population live in ignorance and when the Special Force shows up, we'll be completely unprepared? If we did that, the Special Force would sneak in under our noses like they did in Big Brother. We need to nip them in the bud before they even set a foot in the door. We need numbers in order to defend ourselves. We can't do this alone."

"Did you guys agree to this?" I asked Jan, Glynis and Torvald.

"We tried to fight alone in Big Brother and where did it get us? In jail, in Exile or merged." Torvald spoke for the first time in hours.

"Shifting is the only thing that saved us," Glynis added. "This time that won't be enough."

"They're right," Lina-2 stated. "Everyone needs to know."

"We called Constable Perry. We did a press conference."

"For what?" My stomach twisted.

"We went to the media. They needed proof that what we're claiming is real. I showed them the plugs. Jan and Glynis shifted into the dungeon and back again to prove we were telling the truth."

"I never pictured this happening."

"Lina, you are not supposed to be in control of what happens."

"Then who is?" I backed up until I hit the door.

I felt dizzy. Things were happening too fast. My mind never envisioned ever leaking this information. I thought we could all just live our lives here and pretend nothing was wrong, even if it meant I had to die to keep the peace. Now I saw a different picture. I saw a paranoid world where people were always preparing for war. I saw Carmen's world, where nothing was normal.

"You just handed off our freedom to the government again. Once they are onboard, they'll take over. They'll make us all join the military. There will be an inquisition to root out any spies. We'll never get to have what we want. We'll be trapped just like we were in Big Brother. I'm trying to bring you guys here to save you, not to have you turn around and waste what I've done."

"Lina," my clone shouted, "listen to yourself. You are just mad because you didn't think of it first."

"What?" Lina-2 is disagreeing with me? How could she?

"You can't have what you want. And if you don't fight, your kids won't have what they want either. You can't save everyone—"

"In every reality," I finished. "I *know*."

"That means you can't save us." She reached out and grabbed my shoulders. "This is too big to save one person at a time. We need to secure Safe Place for future generations. Otherwise no one will ever be free."

"Sounds like a Remembrance Day ceremony and you've dubbed us as fallen soldiers."

"If that's what it takes," she said.

I looked at all the people in the room. We weren't the only set of friends in the world. If I were willing to shift to Exile for them, then other people would do the same for their friends. I had to give them that chance.

"Okay. You're right. It's just hard to admit it. I didn't want to live like this. I didn't want to have a war, I just wanted to escape, that was Gerome's plan, but it won't be mine."

Lina-2 hugged me. Everyone hugged me.

"United Defenders it is." I gave them all a salute. It felt appropriate. Then I shifted back to Garden of Eden.

Like my friends in Safe Place, Carmen had changed our plans while I was away. She had recruited a couple hundred people to gather seaweed from the Pacific and fly it back to the colony. Others were asked to weave together a huge seaweed net. It was thirty metres wide and spread across a large lawn close to the medical centre. Hundreds of black plugs were fastened into it, every one of them assigned to one location— the Garden of Eden.

"This way, you won't need arms and legs to shift back," Carmen explained. "No matter what your form is, you'll still have an imprint, but a plug still has to touch it, so it's not guaranteed."

"Who are those people?" I asked, pointing to other groups who were looking on.

"Those are medical personnel standing by to assist those who make it out. And those people are volunteers, who are ready to come in after you if you don't get back."

"That would be too dangerous. I don't need anyone to risk their lives for me."

"Lina," Carmen said, "let them do their job. One of you is not enough."

"Okay." Knowing I had back up should have reassured me. I had a better chance of making it back. Instead, it put me under more pressure to succeed so that I wouldn't put anyone else at risk.

A couple of hours later the net was finished. There was no point to waiting any longer. People dressed in white and grey coats gathered around the net, but none close enough to touch it.

"We are all hoping this will work," Carmen said. "Especially me. I want to see you again."

"I want to see me again. Carmen, thanks for helping me."

"Helping you is helping us all. We'll give you twenty minutes before we start sending people after you."

I took a deep breath. I picked up the edge of the net and held onto it tightly with both hands. Everyone was watching me with worried expressions on their faces. Nobody spoke.

I took another breath. "Take me to Exile."

Chapter 26

I was immobile. Trapped in a suspended state of being. My surroundings were dark and cold. I felt like I was wearing a giant ball gown made of rubber that prevented me from moving or lifting my arms, or even opening my eyes. I thought I was in the wrong place. This didn't feel like an ocean. It didn't feel like anything.

I realized I wasn't breathing. I didn't need to. I didn't have any lungs. Something thick and cold was pressing in around me, pushing me sideways, and I couldn't stop it. I tried to swim, but my legs were useless. They felt long. Really long, like the tail of a kite, swaying in the current.

I couldn't see or hear or smell, but I could taste. Not with a mouth, but right through my skin. I could taste salt. Without some of my senses, I was picking up other factors of awareness. I could feel the presence of other beings. Mostly they felt like beings of my own kind, but something wasn't right. They were animals, simple and crude. They had no intelligent thought, only instinct. They didn't recognize me and I didn't recognize them. They had been here too long to retain any of their humanness. I wondered how long it would take me to completely become an animal.

A pull in the current sent an alarm up to my brain. Something was moving fast. I tried to move. My legs were still useless. Other beings around me were fleeing by pushing themselves up through the pressing substance enveloping them. It was like digging in a tunnel. I stiffened my body, arching upwards. The skirt of my dress spread out and became a parachute. But it wasn't a dress. It was my skin. I stiffened again and shot upwards. I could swim. I was a jellyfish.

So this was Exile. I could not imagine how shocked a person would be if they suddenly morphed into this without warning. I knew what was coming and I still couldn't grasp it. I couldn't accept these new disabilities. I felt trapped.

The current pulled again. Something big was swimming close to me. A feeling of panic filled me and I pushed myself away from the predator. The unknown creature brushed against my tentacles and I stung him. Some of my skin peeled off, not in a painful way, more like scratching a good itch. It rubbed onto the creature's body. Then it swam away.

I'd had jellyfish stings before and they were not pleasant. Blooms of jellies lived off the cost of Victoria. Swimming in the ocean always posed a risk. Some species were fatal. Judging by my size and shape, I guessed I was a purple lion's mane jellyfish. My sting had bite.

My training with Gerome probably helped me to pick up my swimming abilities fast. It could almost be fun if I didn't feel such a strong sense of urgency. I needed to get back to Carmen before I lost my mind. Where had the net gone? What if it didn't shift with me? Would I be stuck here forever?

I had to sense my surroundings with only taste, touch and instinct, but I really needed to see. Instead, I had to rely on an intuition that I had not yet honed. Something bumped into me. It was a gentle touch, like two bubbles of wax in a lava lamp. It was another jellyfish. I was in a bloom of gelatinous zooplankton. They were pushing their bodies toward me and I was beginning to feel crowded. I sensed that they were coming to me on purpose. If the net were close by, it would shift a lot of us.

If the net was below me, it would be sinking to the ocean floor. I relaxed my "skirt" and let myself sink, hoping the other jellyfish would follow me. They did.

My mind wandered, distracted by a growing comfort of my new state. I began tasting the water around me, looking for food. I had to resist the urge to wander off. The connection grew stronger and I didn't like it. I guessed I had been in Exile for fifteen minutes. I was running out of time and jellyfish sink very slowly.

Then, through my skin, I tasted seaweed. Lots of it. The net was lying out on the bottom of the ocean. My tentacles were the first to touch it. I thought I would have to worry about my imprint. Where was it if I no longer had a neck?

"Lina." Carmen shook my shoulder. I realized I had eyes again and opened them. I had fallen to the ground, my body felt as heavy as lead. I was soaking wet, lying on top of jumbled, seaweed net. The temperature was below freezing.

"It worked?" I asked.

She nodded and put a blanket over me as I struggled to sit up. I weighed as much as a truck. My legs were paralyzed from gravity's pull on them. With great effort, I worked the muscles and made them move.

About twenty other people lay there, shivering and groaning with their eyes closed. Their arms and legs did not move. They acted like beached whales.

"Do you know what's wrong with them?" Carmen asked.

"We were jellyfish. They aren't used to their body weight. They haven't used their brains in a while. The longer they were in there, the worse it will be."

"They're going to need rehabilitation. Let's put them in tubs of water." Carmen stood up and gave instructions to the people giving aid. I watched as they scanned the survivor's necks to find out their identity. Then they lifted the ex-sea creatures off the net and carried them inside the medical centre.

"I need new glasses. Whatever they morphed into, they dropped off of me." I rubbed my temples to ward off an oncoming headache. "Carmen, tell me the names of all of the survivors."

She read the list. None of the names sounded familiar.

"There are more. Lots more. I need to go again." I stood up. My balance was bad. Blood rushed to my brain.

"Oh, no, you shouldn't. There are other volunteers." She steadied me. A tall man came over ready to be the next to shift. It was Constable Perry.

"You're a police officer," I said.

"Security Officer," he corrected me.

"I know you. In another reality."

He smiled. "We'll have a chat when this is all over."

"Put the net on top of you this time. It sinks if you don't," I advised him.

As soon as every survivor was cleared off the net, Perry crouched down and pulled the net over his head. Everyone backed away and he was gone.

In under a minute he was back. Eleven other people were standing under the net. They all appeared to be sleeping while they were standing up. Then they all dropped onto the ground in a heap.

"I don't even know what happened," Perry sat up and spoke. "I couldn't feel anything."

A few fish and other sea life must have been touching the net when it shifted and they lay scattered among the humans. Carmen made a quick decision and had them gathered up. Whatever was edible was sent to the kitchens.

"We'll have to feed these people," she said.

I walked through the survivors, looking for anyone I knew, but I saw no one. No Spencer, no Torvald. I called to Carmen. "We need a bigger net."

"We'll keep going until we find everyone."

I looked back at the survivors as they were carried off. So these were the *undesirables*. There didn't seem to be a pattern. They had been condemned for their corrupt DNA. Well, whatever corrupt judgement deemed them undesirable was nothing I could visibly perceive. These were normal-looking people. Maybe they were short or balding or had bad skin, but nothing that justified such brutal discrimination. My resolve against the Special Force strengthened.

"Lina, you need to get off the net. We are ready to go again," Carmen called.

The next volunteer was one of her clones.

"Good luck," I said.

"Thanks."

Carmen told me the names of the second batch of survivors. One of them I had heard somewhere before.

"Wait. Say that last one again."

"Clive Navien."

"I know that name. I think he's one of the students from Young Adult Collegiate." I turned to Carmen's clone. "Go."

The tension was overwhelming and I squeezed my eyes closed. I didn't see Carmen's clone shift. I pinched the bridge of my nose. My headache escalated. I was suddenly weak—too weak even to hold up my arm. It slumped from my face and I sat down before I fell.

"What's wrong?" It was Carmen's voice.

"What's wrong with you?" The voice changed into a demanding, male voice. An old, grouchy voice. Arter's voice.

I flew my eyes open. Arter's face was right in front on me, his loose neck skin, jiggling as he came toward me. I screamed.

"Lina."

I blinked. It was Carmen.

"Whoa." My strength returned to me. I rubbed my eyes. "Sorry, I must be seeing things. It's getting late."

Carmen looked sceptical. "I don't like this. Maybe there are adverse side effects to shifting to Exile. We need to take a closer look at this."

She wanted to take me to the medical centre, but I didn't want to go. I wanted to stay and find Torvald. I wanted to help. As soon as she pulled me to my feet, the net reappeared, filled with over fifty people. The aides called for help and we ran over to offer assistance. We got so busy, I forgot all about my peculiar episode.

I stayed outside until late into the night, waiting for the bodies of my friends to end up on the net. Twice we had to pause to repair the seaweed where it was barely holding together. Still, Spencer and Torvald hadn't shown up. They kept working in shifts, bringing in Exile survivors. The medical centre filled up and they starting filling up the labs. By midnight, they were putting temporary cots in the mess hall.

I acquired a new pair of RAS glasses and continually checked the identification of the incoming Exile survivors as soon as their imprints were scanned. I felt useless standing there, waiting for the net to catch my friends. After a while, I went to the mess hall to see what I could do to help.

Chapter 27

The survivors were in different states of mind. Some were able to sit up and talk as their memories slowly came back to them. Those people hadn't been in Exile for long, maybe a few weeks. Others were a whole lot worse off. They couldn't sit up. They couldn't even open their eyes. I received the assignment of assessing each survivor's level of ability. The group labelled *low concern* stayed in the mess hall until they recovered. As soon as they were ready, they were offered either a position at the colony or a plug back to their own reality. Whatever they chose, they were first invited to donate their DNA.

"Hello, sir, can you tell me your name?" I asked an older man.

He was sitting up with his eyes open, but he remained silent. I scanned his imprint. His name was Levi O'Brian.

"Levi? Is that your name?"

He opened his mouth but what came out was slurred and indistinguishable. He waved his arms around and touched his mouth.

"Can you speak?"

He looked right at me and shook his head. At least he understood me. That was a good sign.

"Do you know what happened to you?"

He shook his head again.

A nurse appeared. "How is this one?"

"He can't speak, but I think he is of low concern." The low-concern label appeared in my glasses just from what I said.

She looked at him, shined a flashlight in his eyes. "Well, having no power of speech should be transferred to high concern. You can help me wheel him over to the Medical Centre." His label switched.

"I don't think so. I mean, no. This man has never been able to speak."

Levi nodded and touched his mouth again.

"See, he's using some sort of sign language."

Levi clapped his hands and smiled.

"Low concern," the nurse stated and walked off. Levi's label changed once more.

"I don't think she likes people questioning her judgment," I said to him.

He grinned.

I smiled back. "Stay here and get some rest. You'll be fine."

I was about to move on to the next patient when my glasses filled with a new list of survivors caught in the net. Torvald flashed brightly.

"Oh my gosh." I dropped my scanner and tripped over the corner of a cot, banging my knee as I hit the floor. Scrambling to my feet, I dashed out of the crowded mess hall.

I made it out to the net, out of breath and shaking in anticipation. I scanned the area. Huge spotlights were illuminating the dark night. The extraction process was well organized and efficient. The net constantly received repairs with new seaweed flown in from the coast. Blankets, cots and personnel continued to arrive with shipments from other colonies to deal with the growing numbers of survivors. By now, it was at least four o'clock in the morning.

Torvald was on his side, flopping around like a fish out of water. I ran up to him and grabbed a hold of him.

"What's wrong with him?" I asked the closest helper.

"He's not the first one to act like this. A few people must have been turned into fish." The guy laughed. "Don't worry. He'll be fine."

I helped him load Torvald onto a gurney and wheeled him into the mess hall. He stopped convulsing by the time we got there.

"What the hell happened to me?" He clapped his hand to his forehead and winced. He still had bruises from those imbeciles beating him up. "That was so not cool."

"Hey, good to have you back." I wrapped a blanket around him and hugged him, but he acted as if he didn't know me.

He looked at his hands and wiped his face with them. "Sick, I'm all wet." He felt the split in his lip where he had hit his face on the concrete. Carefully sitting up and looked around, he took in the makeshift medical camp with hundreds of beds lined in rows, filling the entire mess hall. It was a war-torn Exile refugee camp.

"What is going on here? And what am I wearing?" He pulled at the grey and white fabric clinging to his skin.

I smiled. "For being a fish for three days, you are recovering very well."

He finally recognized me. "Lina." He stood up to hug me and then sat back down before he fell. "Ugh, head rush. You're okay? Those idiots didn't get you?"

"No. I left them all floating in space."

"What do you mean floating in space?"

"I mean, they're dead."

He inhaled sharply. "Did you kill 'em?"

"Not on purpose."

"They used me as bait to find you. I hate that. I'm not bait." He paused. "Were all of these people fish too?" He looked out over the crowded mess hall.

"Some of them. I was a jellyfish."

"You went into Exile?" He looked in my eyes.

"Yeah, to find you. It's taken hours. All of these other people were rescued in the meantime."

"You're a doll, Lina. So...where am I?"

"It's called the Garden of Eden. It's hidden from the Special Force. They do shift back and forth to a reality that is at war with the Special Force. Mostly they fight out in space. I've seen their vessels. They are super neat. You don't have an alternate here, so don't worry. You didn't merge. You can stay here or I can get you a plug back to our home reality."

"No way, I don't want to go back there. Not ever. Too many crappy things happened to me." Torvald appeared to be hiding his fear by concentrating on working his finger muscles and stretching his arms, gaining control of his human form.

"I've got to tell Glynis. She'll be so relieved. She'll want to shift over here so badly."

"I think I ate someone." Torvald's face turned green. "I was starving and I couldn't help it. I ate some minnows." He gasped. "What if they were exiled humans? It could have been someone I know. It could have been *you*."

I wanted to laugh, but I could see that he was seriously grief stricken. I put my arm around his shoulder. "I'm sure no humans were transformed into minnows."

"Ouch, you're hurting me." He brushed my arm off his shoulder and pulled his shirt down to reveal the skin underneath. His entire shoulder was marked with a bright red patch on it.

"Looks like a jellyfish sting," I said. "That was probably me."

The memory of stinging something came into my mind. I felt the peeling sensation as small nodules brushed off my skin, bursting and releasing the poison inside. The memory was so strong I could no longer see Torvald. I was back in my jellyfish body, my tentacles stinging other aquatic animals and eating them by absorbing them through my skin. I was reliving another alternate memory. I should have guessed that an alternate of mine already existed in exile. Now we had merged. Because of my lack of human tendencies, I had the impression this alternate had been in Exile for months, even years. I questioned how I got stuck there and the answer came immediately in another vision.

I saw four hooded men holding flashlights and throwing plugs at me as I struggled to free myself from the chair. The unsteady beams of light revealed a cavern completely built of rocks with a hole in the ceiling and a hole in the floor. The rustling fabric of their black robes flew up as each arm flung another plug. What reality was this? Was I always getting into trouble? Panic built up in my chest. I pulled against the ropes, but they held strong. In slow motion a plug came flying at me, hit my neck and I screamed.

"Lina." Torvald was slapping my cheek, trying to wake me. I had fallen onto the floor of the mess hall. My body felt like deadweight, just like when I shifted out of Exile. A nurse came over.

"I don't know what happened. She just blacked out," Torvald said.

"I think you need some sleep, dear. You've been here all night." The nurse patted my cheek. "There will be another shift along shortly. You've done enough. Go, get some rest."

Torvald pulled me up and trucked me off to an empty cot.

Before I had a chance to lie down, my glasses lit up with the next batch of survivors caught in the net. Spencer Wright was at the top of the list.

"Wait. It's Spencer." I stumbled off the cot and went out to the net. Torvald followed right behind me.

Spencer did not look good. He was on a gurney with a blanket tucked around his still body. He was breathing, but he wasn't moving. He was practically in a coma.

"Hey, Spence." I touched his cheek.

He made no response. His jaw was slack and he looked thin. His hair grew out past his eyes and clumped in big drippy knots across his forehead.

"What's wrong with him?" Torvald asked.

"He's been in Exile for a really long time." I calculated in my head. "Eight months. It looks to me like the amount of time spent in Exile is approximately equal to the amount of time it takes to recover. Torvald, you are exceptionally quicker than most, but Spencer, well, he looks like he's paralyzed."

"I'll take him straight to the Medical Centre." Torvald grabbed one end of the gurney. "You go get some sleep."

I was reluctant to obey.

I watched as he wheeled the gurney away.

Glancing away, I saw a glow on the horizon where dawn was about to break. Billowing clouds tinged with red and violet hovered overhead. A light, misty rain began to fall. Breathing in the fresh smell gave me a second wind. I had things to do. Sleeping could wait.

"Back up," someone yelled. They were about to shift the net again. Another new volunteer crawled underneath and the whole thing vanished. I whispered to my glasses and was gone.

Chapter 28

Something was wrong. It was six in the morning when I shifted back to Safe Place. Jan, Glynis and Lina-2 should have been in bed sleeping, but the dorm was empty. I knew something was worse than wrong when my RAS glasses wouldn't work.

"Show me Jan Kurauchi," I whispered, but the glasses did nothing. I tried the others with the same blank results. Maybe they had all shifted. In that case, my own status should still work. "Show me my shifting history." The glasses were as empty as air. It could only mean one thing. The network with RAS was broken. RAS was no longer in this reality.

Someone had done my job for me, but who? And if RAS hadn't been taken to Exile, where did it go?

I snuck down the stairs and out to the boys dorm. The grounds were absolutely silent. I climbed up the trellis to Yusef's window and peered inside. No one was there either. I pulled myself into the room and peered down the hall. Surely, someone would be up by now. There had to be a couple of keeners studying or working out. A few of the guys' doors were ajar and I peeked inside. Nobody. Not a single soul. The entire place was deserted. The florescent lights flickered in the empty hallway. My throat tightened. I leaned my head against the wall, banging it a couple of times. What happened?

I was exhausted. I hadn't slept all night and my body was getting sluggish, sick with all of the abuse I'd put myself through in the last couple of days. I fought the temptation to just curl up and sleep.

A feeling of loneliness overcame me, making me unbearably depressed. I wanted to burst into tears for no reason. My vision blurred and I refocused inside the cell of a prison.

"Caught you at last," a gruff voice echoed down the hall.

I jumped and whirled around to see who it was. An old man in a long, black robe stood at the end of the hall. Principal Arter again. He floated toward me like a terrifying spectre. The lights began flickering on and off rapidly. Clouds of darkness oozed out of him like smoke. I tried to scream, but my mouth wouldn't open. It couldn't open. I was gagged and tied to a motel bed. Arter was throwing plugs at me. They came at me in slow motion, growing bigger, taking on the shape of large boots. They came zooming up to my face until they completely filled my vision. A hundred black boots in my face.

"No!" I shouted.

The gag was gone. I was lying on the floor in the hallway, the lights jerking back on. I glanced around me. Empty. I was having visions and nightmares that I couldn't control, scared to close my eyes in case Arter came back.

Going back to Yusef's room, I looked for a message or a clue, but none of the paper on his desk was a note to me of any kind. No evidence of a struggle, although his coat was gone. That was a good sign. The Special Force wouldn't have let him get his coat. It meant he left voluntarily and on purpose.

Yusef's computer was hibernating, the laser sensor on his mouse blinking. I went over and turned on the screen. Usually he had it password protected, but it was still logged on. Knowing Yusef, he wouldn't leave his computer logged on unless he was leaving it for somebody to use it. Maybe that somebody was me. I pulled the chair closer to the desk.

I clicked on his browser history and found a news site with a heading entitled, *Should We be Afraid of the Special Force?* The article told me that the school had been evacuated in order to keep the students safe while they rooted out spies. It talked about how the country was in a panic over the testimonies of four students. I skipped to the next webpage. It was a site about the construction of the Alberta Museum. The next site was Yusef's Facebook page. He had an upcoming event titled, *She'll be comin' 'round the mountain,* posted on his wall. *Date: November 30. Place: Wild West.*

November 30? I had to check the calendar because I'd lost track of what day it was. November 30 was today. Yusef had left me a message after all.

"Thanks, smarty pants," I muttered.

I remembered the shoebox under his bed. It was still there with all of the plugs inside. All of them except for the one to the Wild West. Of course, they would go somewhere Torvald wouldn't have to merge. It was the only reality that we knew for sure was safe—and RAS free. But how was I supposed to get there? I emptied the box onto the bed and looked through the plugs. Gerome's handwriting was scrawled across the six digit numbers, giving the plugs scratchy nicknames, Bountiful, Paradise, Playground, Storm, Downtown, Squats, Occupied—they gave a very vague idea of what the reality was actually like—Boredom, Tundra, Purgatory, Machine, Campground, Wilderness, Glamour.

If I could find a reality with another RAS, theoretically, my glasses would start working again. Then I could shift to Wild West—which one should I pick? I banged my head on the wall again, and then pinched the bridge of my nose. Since Gerome had labelled all of these, I could assume he had been to all of them. That meant they were at least somewhat safe.

I began eliminating ones that gave me a yucky feeling. Bulldozer, Clear-cut, Purgatory. Then I took out ones that were probably too primitive to have computers. Squats, Wilderness, and Blizzard.

I narrowed it down to three. Occupied, Control and Doorjamb. I got them ready in my hands so I could shift out easily if it was dangerous. I left an RSVP to Yusef's event invitation—it confirmed that "Halina is attending"—then I closed the screen.

"I hope this works," I whispered to myself. Then I touched the plug to my neck and everything around me changed.

Occupied. 849662.

The room grew very cold. I saw snow on the carpet. The window was busted out and the walls were smudged and crumbling. The dorms were falling apart. I looked through the hole in the wall where the window was missing. I could see the girls building next door in far worse shape. It was bombed out. One exterior wall was ripped away, exposing the rooms inside. Snow had settled on beds and desks. The sky was grey with a blanket of smoke. I could hear gunfire somewhere in the background.

I shook my head and concentrated on my glasses. I asked a few questions, but they didn't light up. No luck. Time to move on. I held up the next plug.

Control. 254359.

"Hey! Where did you come from?" a masculine voice shouted at me.

I whirled around to see a young man stepping out of the bathroom, wearing nothing but a towel. I jumped, dropping the shoebox and spilling the plugs onto the floor.

"*Ack.* Sorry." I stooped down, shielding my eyes and scooping up the plugs as quickly as I could. *Duh, Lina*, I thought, *you're in someone's bedroom.* Not the smartest place to shift. What was I thinking?

"Excuse me, can you leave now?" the guy said.

I tested my glasses with no results.

"Most definitely," I answered and shifted. Too bad I didn't get to see the look on his face when I vanished right in front of him.

Chapter 29

Doorjamb. 556102.

An alarm sounded. I jumped to my feet, scanning the room for any danger. I realized the noise was coming from a clock beside my bed. I looked around and saw shelves filled with swimming trophies, paintings I had done in middle school and a photograph of Jan, Glynis and I at summer camp when we were fifteen. A humming bird hovered at the feeder outside the window. I was wearing my pink pyjamas. I was in my parent's house in Victoria.

"Oh, crap."

If I was here, it meant I had merged with an alternate. An alternate who never went away to Edmonton to attend YAC. At least my alternate had had a full night's sleep. That made me feel a bit better.

"Halina. Your alarm clock is still ringing. Are you awake?" It was my mother outside my door.

Crap. I was about to give my parents another missing daughter.

I looked at the clock. 7:00 am. Friday. I hit the snooze button.

"I'm up," I called. I rushed over to the door and flung it open. My mom was standing there. I gave her a giant hug.

"What was that for?" she asked.

"I love you, Mom."

"I love you too." She smiled. "Halina, your eyes look horrible and why are you wearing glasses?"

The glasses. I couldn't test them in front of her. "They're new," I stammered.

"Okay," she said slowly, looking me over. "Well, get dressed and come downstairs for breakfast."

She walked away and my heart sank, thinking about what I was about to do to her. I closed my door and spoke to the glasses.

"Show me my status."

Halina Pawlak

Location: 556102

Status: Shifter

They worked. Oh, no, they worked. I had to warn my parents. I got dressed in some cool clothes that I didn't remember buying. And made sure I had a high-necked sweater to hide my imprint. I put on enough make-up to cover the fading purple shadows under my eyes. When I pulled on a new pair of socks, I noticed my feet were scaly with eczema or something, but they didn't feel sore when I rubbed them. Just one more problem I had to ignore until this inter-dimensional mess got cleaned up. I found my backpack. It had a couple of textbooks in it that I replaced with the plugs from the shoebox. I went downstairs.

The kitchen was just how I remembered it. The lace curtains were open, showing the hollyhocks swaying in the breeze. It was hard to imagine that anything was wrong.

"Mom, do you remember that school in Edmonton called Young Adult Collegiate?"

"Halina, we've been through this before." She eyed me as she pulled milk out of the fridge.

"We have?"

She set the milk on the table. "You're at U of Vic because they have better programs and better systems. We didn't want you going to some experimental school where the structure has never been tested. This is such an old argument, Halina, why are you bringing it up again?"

"I'm not arguing. I've heard some really bad stuff about YAS recently." I poured myself some cereal.

"Like what?" My dad came into the room, wrapping his tie around his neck. I jumped up and hugged him too.

"I heard that the real reason they have that school is to weed out people that they feel are unfit for society and get rid of them. It is totally unfair and you have to do something."

"Where did you hear this?" He sat down. "I haven't heard anything about this."

"It's a conspiracy. The government might be involved. I think I'm in trouble." It wasn't a complete lie. I *was* in trouble. My parents were going to need the lead because, according to this reality, I was about to go missing. "There is a secret society named the Special Force that is trying to create a superior race. I spoke out against them and now they are after me."

"What? What do you mean they are after you?" Dad asked.

"I mean, it's a bad idea for me to go to school today."

"But you have to go. You have an exam." My mother denied the truth in my remarks.

I wanted to prove to them that I wasn't making it up. I wanted them to believe me. I was tempted to show them my glasses. Show them that the Special Force might be sneaking into this world. I just didn't have the time to deal with their freak out right now. I had to make it to the Wild West and find my friends. I had to go.

"Okay, I'll go, but don't say I didn't warn you."

I got up and went. As soon as I was out of sight, I snuck into the garage. My parents and the Victoria police were going to have a busy night tonight. Once they realized I was gone, they would need a lot of help. Little good it would do. I was about to cause another mysterious disappearance. Then I had a brilliant idea. My clones. If Lina-2 was covering for me at Safe Place, another Lina could be sent here. When this mess was over, I resolved to give my parents their daughter back.

I was more worried about why my glasses were working. Where was the RAS computer here and who had control of it? I would make sure I gave my clone a mission to find out. I could kill two birds with one stone.

Last thing I felt I would miss was my new turtleneck. I hugged the collar once before I shifted.

Chapter 30

I was under the stairs in Mr. Aims's trading post. Rough wooden beams supporting each stair creaked from the weight of someone climbing up to the attic. Small streams of dust fell between the planks. My glasses were the shape of old fashioned spectacles. I was sitting on a tattered quilt, wearing a cheerful rose patterned dress and matching bonnet. Ugh. I missed the turtleneck already.

I looked around. Yusef wanted to meet me at the museum. If it existed in this reality, it would be right here. So where was he? I assumed the person who just went upstairs was Mr. Aims. The clan wouldn't go out in public, would they? It was then I noticed a large rock sitting at my feet. Where had that come from? I hefted the boulder into my hands. It weighed about six kilograms. I turned it over and saw three letters carved into the back—RAS. This was the computer.

I chuckled. Just as Torvald had predicted. The computer was chiselled into a rock.

The next question I asked myself was why was it left here? Where was everybody? I had to find them. Pulling up my bulky, rosy skirt, I crawled out from under the stairs. Time to find Yusef. Rounding the corner into the back room, I came face to face with a double-barrelled shotgun.

"They said you'd be droppin' by." Mr. Aims's greasy, black comb-over slid to one side. The gun shook in his hands.

I pulled the bonnet off my head so I could see better. I wasn't scared of him. He was a small man with an even smaller voice.

"Now what else you hidin' back there?" he squeaked.

"Nothin', sir. Honest."

"Don't be smart with me, missy." He peered over my shoulder. "What's in that knapsack? Some of your voodoo magic?" He reached for the kerchief full of plugs and through it aside. "You better come up to the front o' the shop with me. Someone's been waiting for ya."

I hoped it was my friends, the Unified Defenders.

No such luck.

A man stood in the shadows. I recognized his stubbly jowls and drooping lips, half hidden under his black-rimmed hat. Arter, the scum of every reality, draped in a black poncho and jingling leather boots.

I eyed the henchmen with him. They were alternates of the same four guys I had left to freeze out in space. Hill-Billy's grin was as wide as an ocean.

"Miss Pawlak, you have been causing me much grief." Arter's voice was low, controlled. "Such a waste of my time." He lifted his baggy eyes to meet mine. "Anything to say for yourself?"

"Yeah, you look ridiculous."

Mr. Aims jabbed the gun into my back. "Watch it, missy."

"So typical of a slacker like you to criticize surface appearances and never address the real issue." Arter sneered at me. "This isn't the first time we've had to deal with your kind. You and all of your alternates have been pestering us in reality after reality. Tyler thought he could control you this time. He's tried before. He just wanted to keep you all to his little self. Since he never returned to us, I suspect his plan failed once again."

My voice caught in my throat. Did I understand him correctly? Did I have other alternates who were also fighting him? Of course I did. Every alternate I had would act the same, make the same decisions and have the same feelings.

"Every time I run into you, I think, naw, this girl won't be a threat. Not this time. She's just a kid. This time she'll mind her own business. But I underestimate you every time. Looks to me like I've got to stop giving you second chances. Get rid of you as soon as I find you. I'm just gonna have to Exile you like I've had to do before. I've sent four of you there so far. I imagine they've all merged into some slimy sea creature. One more, Miss Pawlak? "

I stared at him, realizing what was wrong with me. That's why I'd had all those crazy black outs. When I went to Exile, I merged with four of my alternates all at once. My brain was on overload. I was shoving a swimming pool full of memories into a water balloon and hoping it wouldn't burst. I couldn't even blame him for it, since I'd gone there voluntarily on a rescue mission—a mission Arter would be delighted to hear about.

"Exile? Ha. I've already been there, big deal. You should go there sometime, although these days you might find the ocean a bit empty. Pretty devoid of any—how did you put it—slimy sea creatures. Not following me? Let me explain. I went into Exile and rescued *everybody in there.*"

The look on his face was comical. His eyes popped out of his head even further than they already were. Then his face turned red with rage.

"You've crossed me for the last time, Miss Pawlak. There are other ways to get rid of you. Permanent ways." He nodded to his henchmen. "String 'er up, boys."

Chapter 31

The henchmen hooted, hollered and then dragged me outside. They pulled my shoes off.

"That's so you can't run away." One of them said. Then he tied my hands behind my back. "And this is so you can't crawl away."

Hill-Billy laughed. "Time to meet yer maker." He strung a rope over one of the front porch beams. One end of the rope was a hangman's noose.

Some of the townspeople stepped over, but Arter stepped into the street and pushed them back. "Stay back or you're next," he threatened.

I frantically searched the eyes of the growing crowd. Would nobody help me? I scanned the faces of the people, willing myself to recognize someone, anyone, but these pioneers and cowboys were useless to me. The only souls with any confidence at all were the bawdy women leaning over the hotel balcony, winking at Arter. He blew a kiss at them. Sick.

"Any last words?" Hill-Billy asked, as he pulled the noose over my head and tightened it around my neck.

Rough hemp fibres dug into my skin. I gagged. Standing on my bare toes at the edge of the boardwalk, I struggled to keep my balance. How many times had I perished by the hands of the Special Force? How many Linas were left to continue the struggle? I wanted to despair, knowing I had lost again. But however hopeless my situation was, I couldn't appear defeated. If I was about to die, I would go out with a bang.

"Yeah, I do have something to say. Good luck with your pitiful cause." I gave him a mocking smile. "You'll never succeed. There are too many people like me who will do everything to stop you. With Exile empty and all of your prisoners free, I've just added thousands more fighters to the United Defenders."

"The United Losers is more like it. Good bye, missy." He reached out to push me off the porch, but the rope mysteriously broke and dropped off the beam. It flopped onto the boardwalk like a harmless dead snake.

I shuddered with a sigh of relief.

"What the—"

The henchmen all tipped their heads up into the sunny sky looking for the cause of the broken noose. Now was the time to fight.

I reached my bare foot out and kicked Hill-Billy. I hit his arm, although I was aiming for his crotch. My foot did something weird. I felt the same peeling feeling I'd had when I was a jellyfish. He let out a squeal and fell flat on his back. He grabbed his arm as if it was on fire. It began to swell and a red blotch spread up to his hand.

How had I retained that power? Since jellyfish were common in most realities, had I kept a part of it? I looked down at my feet and noticed it wasn't eczema, but tiny nodes of venom. When they burst, they didn't sting me. They stuck to whatever they came in contact with. Confidence boiled inside of me. I went into attack mode.

Mr. Aims came to the doorway. "What's with all your hollerin'?"

Hill-Billy pointed a shaking, swollen finger at me. "Sh-she stung me."

"With what?"

"With my voodoo magic." I launched a side kick at Mr. Aims. He caught my foot with his hands, but then let go of it.

"What have you done to me?" He screamed. "I'm being burned alive." Steam rose from his burning hands. He glanced around, his eyes wide with panic, and spotted a water trough for horses. He ran to it and jumped in, screaming like a girl.

I laughed and kicked the next closest man. He threw his hands up to avoid touching me and I hit my mark. Bull's-eye. He keeled over and grabbed his crotch, getting the poison on his hands anyways. The other men backed off when I raised my foot in their direction.

"You cowards," Arter fumed. He jumped back onto the deck.

"But we can't touch her. What d'you expect us to do?"

"Shoot her, you idiots."

They raised their guns.

I was trapped. My only escape was back through the door into the trading post. I dove. Guns went off, sending splinters of the doorframe blasting through the air. I scurried back against the wall to avoid a second round. One man came through the door. I thought I was dead, but before he even crossed the threshold, a bullet hit him in the chest. Blood splashed down the front his shirt as he slumped forward.

"Hold your fire," Arter yelled.

The gunfire stopped.

I wiped the hair out of my face, shaking with adrenaline. I tried to find the mystery shooter, but there was no one in the room with me. Then I remembered the sniper window up by the roof. Sure enough, the barrel of a rifle was poking out of it. Whoever was holding that gun had just saved my life. Probably the same hand that cut the noose. I couldn't see who it was, but my gut told me it was a United Defender. I had to get to the roof.

The attic stairs were in the back room and I would have to cross in front of the doorway to get there. Taking a deep breath to steady my nerves, I crept up to the entrance. Pulling my feet under me, I sprang across the doorway. Gunshots fired both ways through the door. Another of Arter's men went down, clutching the side of his neck. I ran to the stairs, knocking over crates as I went. My hobo stick lay on the floor and I tried to grab for it, but Arter's men came dashing into the front of the store, firing through the metal bars. I leapt up the stairs, the floorboards filled with bullet holes the second I stepped off each one.

Once in the attic, I ran over to the hatch and flung it open with my hands still tied. Boots clomped up the stairs behind me. I jumped through the hatch and slammed it back down. Someone grabbed me from behind and I screamed. I whirled around. It was Yusef. I sunk into his arms. A cowgirl version of Glynis stood close by with a rifle propped on her hip. She was definitely getting her "hands-on experience" now.

"Tell me you have a plug with you," I cried.

"No, don't your glasses work?"

"No."

Thump. Someone was banging on the hatch. The lock on the lid was weakening under the strain. Glynis pointed her rifle, ready to fire.

"There are too many," I desperately yelled.

"Time to go." Yusef pulled us to the edge of the roof.

"Hold on." He leaned over.

A wagon full of hay sat parked in the alley beneath us. Cowgirl Jan was up front, holding the reins with her elk hide mittens, and Cowboy Torvald held a rifle at the ready.

Yusef grabbed my shoulders and threw me into the wagon. A pile of straw protected my bare feet from the fall. Glynis jumped down beside me.

"Go," Torvald yelled to Jan.

She smacked that whip like a pro. The wagon lurched forward and I grabbed the edge for balance.

"Here." Yusef bent down to untie my hands. His fingers lingered on mine. "Are you okay?"

"Yes." His hands were warm even in the frozen air. The ice crystals of our breath mingled together.

He inched closer to me, staring in my eyes, but I pulled myself away when he almost touched my feet.

"Hey, I need a pair of shoes," I yelled. "Glynis. Your boots will fit me. I need them."

"What about me?" she asked.

"I'm sorry, but trust me. My feet need to be covered. You don't want to touch them. They have poison on them."

She removed her cowboy boots and gave them to me.

"How come you get cool clothes and I'm stuck with this fluff?" I ripped the bulky skirt off down to a pair of bright red pantaloons.

Glynis looked down at her leather vest and chaps then looked back at me. "Because I wouldn't be caught dead in that."

I turned to Yusef. "How did you find me?"

"When we saw your reply on Network, we knew you'd be here somewhere and came looking for you."

"Thank you for that. You guys saved my life."

"We need to get back to Safe Place," Yusef explained as the wagon charged toward the river. "We've been recruited to help head up the United Defenders."

"Who's involved?"

"The government, the army, everyone. Once CSIS corroborated our story, things really took off. Apparently, the agency already knew about Special Force and hoped it wouldn't go public. But now that it has, they're helping with preventative preparations."

"So how can we get back?"

"We thought you had plugs," Jan yelled over the thundering of hooves.

"Aims took them all. We'll have to go back." I stood up to see over the edge of the cart. Horses were ploughing their way toward us, their riders in black.

Chapter 32

"They're after us," I yelled. The others stood up. A shot rang out and thumped into the back of the wagon.

"Get down," Torvald commanded as he set his rifle and fired back.

We raced on, bullets flying, our faces red with cold. Buildings made way for trees. We tried to outrun them, but our horses were pulling a heavy wagon and were losing speed. If we could get to the river valley, maybe the slope would lessen their load.

"There's no bridge," Jan cried. Her voice was frantic.

"What about the ferry?" I called.

"It's on the other side."

Of all the crazy situations I'd been in, this was the pinnacle of stupid. The road ahead of us was shrinking rapidly. The river was high and flowing fast. The ferry was just leaving the far shore, breaking through clumps of ice that hung to the rocks. It would never make it to us in time.

"I've run out of bullets." Torvald threw his rifle into the hay.

"Have courage, mates," Glynis yelled as she took over Torvald's post.

The river was right in front of us.

"Hang on," Jan screamed as she pulled hard to the right.

The horses whinnied and banked hard. The wagon went up on two wheels, leaving the road and bouncing onto a pebble sandbar. The henchmen tried to follow us. One horse drove straight into the river. Another reared up and dropped his rider leaving only one left. Arter. He whipped his stallion into a full-on charge.

"Shoot him!" I yelled.

Glynis took aim. Just as she pulled the trigger, the wagon hit a boulder. The jolt bounced the gun out of her hands and tipped the wagon, sending it tumbling into the water. I heard gasps as my friends hit the freezing water. In a weird and shocking revelation, I realized the water felt warm to me—inviting me in like it was my home. Like I could sink under the surface and swim away.

I looked around to survey the damage. One of the lenses of my glasses had a small crack so I pulled them off my face and stuck them in the front of my corset.

Everything seemed to happen at once.

The horses snorted and stopped pulling the toppled wagon. Jan's leg was pinned under the seat, the wet reins still in her hands. Yusef heaved at the cart to free her. Torvald hit his head on a rock and passed out. His body caught the current and slid away. Glynis jumped in after him.

I didn't know who to go to first.

"No!" I reached after Glynis, but she was beyond my grasp. My feet found the river bottom and I sloshed back out. I headed back toward Arter. Back to where Glynis dropped her rifle.

"Lina. What are you doing?" Yusef yelled, trying to catch me.

"I'm exerting confidence even in the face of unlikely odds." I skidded over the gravel and grabbed the rifle with shaking fingers. I clumsily cocked the gun and slanted it up under my armpit.

The horse was snorting with exertion, nostrils flared. Its pounding hooves sprayed up rocks and water.

"Miss Pawlak, your time has come!" Arter yelled. He was psychotic, teeth protruding, spit flying. I could see others catching up behind him. He fired at me, but couldn't hold the gun steady and the shot went wide. He was practically on top of me.

"My turn." I exhaled and fired.

The horse bucked and flipped, landing right at my feet. Arter screamed as he fell on his back into the frozen water. A shard of ice sliced through his neck. He went limp. The river around him turned red.

One of the fallen riders came splashing toward me. "You demon. You'll pay for this."

The other rider remounted his horse and headed for me at breakneck speed. I tried to fire at both riders, but the gun jammed. I threw it down.

Yusef grabbed the sleeve of my muddy shirt and yanked me backward. "Run!" He shoved me toward the wagon.

Jan was already running ahead of us, dragging her left leg. We dodged bullets as we stumbled over the icy rocks. The sandbar ended and the bank sloped. I lost my balance and slid into the water. Yusef dove in after me. The current took us away from the men chasing us.

We caught up to Jan as she picked her way over the shore. Tree branches slapped at her face. She wouldn't be able to keep up with us.

"Jump," I yelled.

Her eyes widened and she gave me an "are-you-serious" look. Glancing over her shoulder at our pursuers, she took a deep breath and jumped. I swam over to her, putting my rescue training into full force.

There. Near the rocks.

Her head rose above the surface and she gasped in a breath of air. Her body was rigid.

"Jan?"

"I c-can't m-move." She choked and gagged on the murky water.

"I've got you." I scooped my arm under her armpits and surveyed the water for Yusef. He was gone.

"Yusef," I screamed.

Downstream, Glynis struggled with a coughing Torvald. I watched as she held him above the surface. The water was up to her chest. "Help us, Lina."

"We're coming," I hollered.

Carrying Jan, I pushed farther into the river and stumbled into them. All four of us lost our footing and sunk into the bitter, frigid river.

Torvald let out a yell. "I'm f-freezing. Get me out of this water."

"Not yet," I snapped. "I have to find Yusef."

Torvald grabbed the girls while I dove under the surface. A weird feeling spread over me. I wasn't cold. It was as though my skin was used to the temperature. It was hard to keep my eyes open in the fast moving water . I thought about my experience in Exile. Without any eyes, I had been able to sense my surroundings. I needed to be able to use that instinct now.

I closed my eyes.

I felt the pull of the water and had the distinct impression another life floated close by. Honing in on the feeling, I began swimming toward the opposite shore. The taste of fish entered my brain. It was working.

"Where are you, Yusef?" I branched out my mind, seeking for evidence of him. Then I felt it. A body was approaching me and it was coming fast. I opened my eyes just as Yusef's unconscious form smacked into me. I grabbed him in a football tackle and pushed off from the riverbed. His head broke the surface. I held him by his collar and slapped his face.

"Wake up." I slapped him again.

He sputtered and choked. His eyes blinked open. "I'm in Exile." He could barely speak. His head went back under.

I pulled him up. "Tread water."

"I can't."

"Yes, you can. You took lessons."

"No, I didn't. I have to shift out of here."

"Yusef." I slapped him a third time.

He looked into my eyes and recognized me. "Lina, you're alive." He hugged me and we both went under.

"What is wrong with you?" I asked when we resurfaced.

He gulped for air. "M-must have m-merged."

He was the Yusef from Big Brother. *My* Yusef. My heart leapt with joy.

"Yusef! Thank goodness. I thought I would never see you." I was laughing and crying while trying to hold him up.

"Let's shift out of here," he pleaded.

A light went on in my head. "You have plugs. Where are they?"

"In my p-pocket with my horseshoe."

"We have to get back to the others. We have to be together."

"Huh?" He looked over my head. "What the—" Water splashed into his mouth and he gagged.

The others called out to us. I grabbed the collar of Yusef's shirt and, panting with exertion, I pulled him toward our friends. As soon as we were all desperately clinging to each other, we planted our feet down hard. Torvald made the best anchor. Grunting with the effort, he pulled against the current. We slowly made our way back to shallow water.

"Jan d-doesn't look so g-good," Glynis stuttered.

Jan's lips were blue and she didn't respond when I called her name. Just as we were gaining good ground, a gunshot rang out and splashed into the water beside us. The two henchmen were catching up to us.

"Get a plug out of my pocket," Yusef begged. "Everyone hang on."

I dunked my head under, grasping at his clothing. I felt the bulky horseshoe and found a plug. Still underwater, I touched it to my neck.

Nothing changed.

Breaking the surface of the water, I was about to ask what happened. But my eyes gave me the answer. The banks of the river appeared the same, covered in thick pine trees, but beyond them rose hundreds of skyscrapers up on the ridge, like the turrets of a great castle. Above us, the LRT Bridge rumbled as the subway shot past. We were back, but where exactly, I had no idea.

Chapter 33

We struggled out of the river and lay on the shore, convulsing with cold, soaked and shivering. I clutched Yusef harder.

Yusef tried to pry me off him. "Lina, it's okay." He pulled me back and looked into my eyes. "It's me, the old me, the real me."

Something clicked inside me. A wave of pent up emotion. An urge for something to be normal again. I don't know if it was out of relief or exhaustion. I grabbed his face and kissed him, hard and desperate, like it was the last kiss of my life.

He pulled back, stunned. I couldn't read his reaction behind those black eyes. He looked different than I had ever seen before.

"Where have you been?" he gently asked, wiping the tears from my cheeks.

"Me? Where have *you* been?"

"Waiting for you." He smiled.

He leaned in, threading his fingers through the back of my hair. It gave me the shivers. It was exhilarating. When our lips touched, it was slow and safe. I dissolved into him. We fused together. He closed his hands around my hair as if he would never let me go. I never wanted him to.

Glynis sat up and tittered in surprise. "Finally."

I pulled away, embarrassed. I noticed I had my cool turtleneck back on. I pulled the collar up over my nose and breathed in. Even though it was soaked with river water, it smelled so much better than my Wild West dress. Yusef also looked and smelled way better.

I rested my head on his chest and sighed. "So where are we?"

Yusef squinted at the plug. "Number 283900. It's called Crush."

"How appropriate," Jan rasped. She winked at me.

Yusef sighed. "You won't believe the things I've been through."

"I bet I can top all of your—"

"I watched you get sent to Exile," he interrupted. "In another reality. I went crazy. Freaked out thinking I might not see you again. That's when I knew how much I wanted to be with you."

I gave him a shaky smile. "My mind is mashed up with six different lifetimes. I can't focus on anything."

"Lina, you don't look good. Are you feeling okay? Is everyone okay?"

Jan slowly got up, limped over and hugged me for warmth. "I'm fine. Just a human popsicle."

Torvald nodded. "Do you know how we can get back? Or where we should go? We need to warm up."

"My glasses might work," I said. "Show me Yusef Hassam."

They lit up. It was a miracle.

"Oh, good." Jan had a tear dripping down her cheek. She pulled Glynis and Torvald up. We gathered in a tight circle.

"Family hug, mates." Glynis smiled.

Yusef stared wide-eyed at my glasses. "Those aren't real, are they? You better tell me where you got those freaky glasses." He pulled a handful of plugs from his pocket and began sorting through them.

"Ha ha, he's forgotten," Torvald cheered. "Show him again. I want to see him pull his hair out."

I closed my hand around his. "We don't need the plugs."

"What?"

"Let me give you a demonstration so you can see just how freaky my glasses really are."

His eyes lit up.

"Take us to Safe Place."

We disappeared.

Message from the Author

Dear Reader,

My high school experience was not an uplifting one for me. I was the constant target of bullying (because I was too skinny, go figure). Being a teen was not easy.

The kinship Lina had with her friends is the kind I always dreamt about. She made clear, conscious decisions about how she would treat her friends. She never abused their trust or broke her promises to them. In that way, maybe I portrayed her as too mature for her age, but I sure wish there were more people like that in this world.

I wanted Lina's group to be varied and diverse, not only ethnically, but intellectually and emotionally. Their interests varied from weight lifting to computers but each person's unique role was edifying and beneficial to their cause. They represented the opposite of the abusive segregation that Arter attempted.

Difference does not equal fear. Diversity does not equal intolerance. We can find hidden talents in everyone, and those talents should be praised. The first time a guy told me I had killer legs I was shocked. I thought I was too skinny because I was constantly told that. I thought I had to look like those girls in magazines. I thought everyone was shallow. But they're not. *I* was judging *them.*

After that, it was so much easier to turn my weaknesses into strengths and forgive the faults of others. I did find them, my ideal group of friends, who pulled me through some pretty tough times and I'll always be thankful to them. They taught me that no one should be excluded. No one should be sent to Exile.

Sincerely,

Halli Lilburn

Discussion Questions

Everyone needs a break from reality every once in a while. The irony is the characters in "Shifters" are doing far more than that. They face not one reality, but several. If you could create your ultimate reality, what would it be?

In Safe Place, Glynis is not a part of Jan's life and we see distinct differences in her personality. How has the influence of one person changed your life? What would you be like without them?

There are many references to water symbolizing the change in Lina's growth and in her relationships. Can you interpret the message behind image of the swimming pool with Coach Tyler? When the pool is drained? In the ocean of Exile? In the river with Yusef?

The phrase 'You can't save everyone in every reality' is mentioned a few times. What does this mean? Who is she able to save and who is beyond saving?

The idea of cloning is a moral issue with arguments on both sides. Should it be allowed? When would it be beneficial for mankind? What could be some of the negative consequences?

School is a central institution in every student's life. Within we are taught to follow rules and obey authority figures. Lina and her friends suffer the consequences of disobedience, but when is their rebellion mere disrespect and when does it become an uprising? When authority oversteps its bounds, are we justified in fighting back? Where is the line and who draws it? Can you see examples of powerful leaders abusing their authority in the world today? Do we as a nation have the obligation to stop them?

About the Author

Halli Lilburn always dreamed of being a published author and SHIFTERS is her first novel.

Halli was born in Edmonton, Alberta, Canada. She currently resides on a small farm somewhere in southern Alberta with her mountain man husband and three genius children. She enjoys painting, singing, sewing and working at the local library.

http://www.hallililburn.blogspot.com

http://www.shifterssaga.blogspot.com

IMAJIN BOOKS

Quality fiction beyond your wildest dreams

For your next ebook or paperback purchase, please visit:

www.imajinbooks.com

www.twitter.com/imajinbooks